THE LAKE

Sheena Lambert is from Dublin, Ireland, where she worked as an engineer on landfill sites before leaving the glamour of waste management behind to focus on writing novels, plays and newspaper articles.

Her writing has been shortlisted in a number of prestigious UK competitions.

Twitter @shewithonee
Facebook: sheenalambertauthor
www.sheenalambertauthor.com

Also by Sheena Lambert

A Gathering Storm (previously *Alberta Clipper*)

SHEENA LAMBERT

The Lake

an imprint of HarperCollins*Publishers*
www.harpercollins.co.uk

Killer Reads
An imprint of HarperCollins*Publishers*
1 London Bridge Street
London SE1 9GF

www.harpercollins.co.uk

This paperback edition 2015
1

First published in Great Britain by
HarperCollins*Publishers* 2015

A catalogue record for this book is
available from the British Library

ISBN: 978-0-00-813475-4

Set in Minion by Born Group using Atomik ePublisher from Easypress

MIX
Paper from
responsible sources
FSC www.fsc.org **FSC® C007454**

FSC is a non-profit international organisation established
to promote the responsible management of the world's forests.
Products carrying the FSC label are independently certified
to assure consumers that they come from forests that are managed
to meet the social, economic and ecological needs
of present and future generations.

Find out more about HarperCollins and the environment at
www.harpercollins.co.uk/green

For John, forever

I hear lake water lapping with low sounds by the shore;
While I stand on the roadway, or on the pavements grey,
I hear it in the deep heart's core.

– W. B. Yeats

ONE

Friday, 26th September 1975

'Frank. Phone call.'

Somewhere between asleep and awake, Frank heard the words barked from behind his bedroom door. It took a second or two before he could open his eyes. Sunlight streamed through the unlined curtains as if they were hardly there at all. The digital clock by the bed flashed 00:00. Frank groped for the wristwatch lying next to it and squinted at it instead. Twenty-five past nine. Who the hell could be calling him? He tried his best not to disturb Rose as he got up from the bed and went out into the hall.

The receiver was cold in his hand. 'Hello?'

'Frank? Is that you?' The lilt in the voice did little to soften its booming depth.

Frank stood a little straighter. 'Yes. Inspector Carter?'

'Yes. Look Frank, I know you have the weekend off, but, well, something's come up.'

Ah Jesus.

'It's a body. And Jason's away. And Eddie … well, I'd just rather you went down there, Frank.'

He pressed his fingers into his eyes. 'Down where, sir?'

1

'Crumm. The local guard is on his own there. The doc will be down later today. Hopefully.'

'Hopefully?'

'Well, there's been another incident in Cork. And this thing in Crumm; it looks like it might only be a bog body. He might have to prioritize Cork. He might not get to Crumm until the morning.'

'Tomorrow morning?'

'Yeah. You'd better pack for the weekend.'

Frank rubbed his castigated eyes again. Rose was going to kill him.

The phone was silent for a moment. 'So when can you get here? I'll have the file ready for you.'

'Right. Okay.' It was freezing in the hall, even though the weather had been warm for weeks. Frank wished he had put on a T-shirt. 'I'll be in by eleven.'

'Okay. Thanks Frank.'

'Sure, sir. No problem.'

Frank was so intent on shutting the door soundlessly that he forgot about the warped floorboard just inside the threshold. Rose's eyes opened, although her head didn't stir from the pillow.

'What was that about?'

'I thought you were asleep.' Frank pulled down the covers and vaulted back into bed, shivering. 'That bloody hall feels like ten below.'

'The phone.' Rose's tone was barely tempered by the pillow half covering her mouth.

Frank turned his head to face her. 'It was work.' He waited a second. He knew he wouldn't have to elaborate.

'Ah Jesus, Frank.' Rose suddenly seemed very awake; her head propped up on one elbow, her apparent disbelief glowering down on him and his pillow. 'Tell me you're not going in?'

'Worse, I'm afraid.' Frank was conscious that the disappointment of this conversation was going to be predominantly one-sided. He turned his head on the pillow and wondered briefly what that meant. Yellowed paint was peeling from a patch of ceiling above their heads. 'I have to go to Crumm. Overnight.' He looked at her again. 'I should be back tomorrow.'

'Should be?' She spoke quickly, but then seemed to check herself. A moment passed before she sat up and swung her legs out of the bed. A stripe across the middle of her back was paler than the rest of her skin. Frank thought it strange that he had never noticed it before. She reached down to the end of the bed and lifted a black T-shirt from where it been discarded, not long after they had come in the previous night.

'You know you promised.' She pulled the T-shirt over her head. 'This weekend. You promised that you would really look.'

She turned and glanced at him, briefly, over her shoulder, before standing up and pulling at her jeans that were lolling over a chair. Frank exhaled and rolled his eyes to the ceiling; throwing his arm up and over his head to touch the buttoned, velour headboard. This seemed to have the effect of speeding her up.

'What can I do, Rose?' He sat up in the bed. 'It's work. You know how it is. If I want to get on, I have to do these things.'

'They own you.'

'Yes, they do.' Frank nodded manically. 'For the moment, they do.'

Rose stopped dressing, and stood at the foot of the bed, staring at him. Frank stared back. She would own him too if she had her way. She pulled a band from the pocket of her jeans and twisted it into her hair. But then her face clouded with a sadness he couldn't bear to see. He patted the bed beside him, and she sat.

'Look,' he lifted his hand to her neck. 'I will get a place. Of my own. And you may paint it whatever colour you desire. And I will designate a drawer in my bedroom for your sole use. And we will have some privacy.'

She looked up from twisting a loosened blanket thread through her fingers. 'And then what?'

3

Frank paused. Then he would almost be thirty, and then it would be ridiculous not to ask her to marry him, and then he would be tied down forever to a life and a person he wasn't convinced he really loved. 'And then we'll see,' he said.

TWO

Peggy stood still for a moment, eyes straight ahead, waiting for the dizziness to abate. Then, with the spent light bulb held, tentatively, in a vice-like grip between her teeth, she lowered her hands, slowly, onto the leather seat of the high stool, bending her knees as she went, mindful of the unevenness of the century old flagstone floor. Crouched in this position, like a sprinter waiting for a gunshot, she paused again, before dismounting. She waited until she was sure she was stable, and then lifted the stool and plonked it back down at the bar with a clatter.

'You should have joined the circus when you had the chance,' a voice from the front door said. Peggy turned and grinned at Maura with the bulb still tight between her teeth.

'You shouldn't be climbing barstools, or changing light bulbs, anyway. Where is that brother of yours when things of that nature need doing?' Maura flicked her duster in the direction of the errant light fitting before closing the door, and taking her apparent displeasure out on the plaques and framed photos of men with fish that adorned the walls of the little porch; her disapproving head rocking all the while in perfect time with her behind.

Peggy flicked an ancient-looking switch on the wall next to her and the new bulb turned white, although it made no obvious contribution to the small square room that was already bright with midday sunlight. She didn't need her brother around to change light bulbs. Or bring in the coal. Or change a keg. Or pull a pint. Or all the other things Maura thought she needed a man for. She cast her eyes around the room, before going behind the bar and stooping to lift Coke bottles from a crate on the floor. She regarded every bottle an amazing feat of engineering and design; positioning each one with reverence on the old wooden shelves. Some were more worn than others, their glass opaque and almost sandy to touch. The odd time you might come across a brand new one. A new little bottle on its first journey. Crumm today; who knew where next? Peggy would hold each new bottle and imagine its next trip to be to a Jurys Hotel, or maybe even the Shelbourne, in Dublin. Peggy liked stocking the mineral shelves. She liked the order to it, the neatness. Although she would never admit it to her siblings. They would laugh at her. Or worse.

'So the village is full of talk of the find.' Maura's voice floated over the bar to where Peggy knelt on the cold floor by the Coke crate. She could tell from Maura's breathlessness that she had started on the windows. 'Do you hear me? Peg?'

'I do.' Peggy clinked two bottles in a sort of wordless signal.

'Mrs. McGowan says that they're sending someone up from Dublin.'

'Yes?'

'A detective, I suppose.' Maura spoke with some reverence. 'Sure they'd have to send someone.'

'They would?'

'Well they could hardly let young Michael deal with it by himself.'

Peggy shook her head at the shelf of bottles. Poor Garda O'Dowd. They'd never give him a chance. He had been a guard for four years now, and they still saw him in short pants. 'I'm sure Garda O'Dowd would be well able to manage,' she offered.

'Huh.' Maura looked over the bar; her grey, lacquered curls defying gravity as she did so. 'He's all right for directing traffic at a funeral, or ordering the stragglers out of this place,' she said, flicking her duster at nothing in particular, 'but a body?' She leant on the bar with the self-assured enlightenment of any of the old men that might take her place in a couple of hours' time. 'I don't think he's cut out for that sort of thing.'

She took herself back to the windows and Peggy resumed emptying the crates and filling the shelves. She could see the wooden uprights beginning to rot where they met the floor close to her knees. The corner of one wobbled in her hand like a child's tooth. She cast her eyes to the ceiling. The plaster had dried out well over the summer, but it was bound to start raining again soon. They should really get the roof tarred while they had the chance. A rare flush of irritation deepened the colour of her naturally rosy cheeks. That was something Jerome could have taken care of. If he were ever here. But no sooner had the thought barged into her head, than she showed it the way out. She would rather climb stools, and pay one of the local lads to tar the roof, than have Jerome here with her seven days a week.

The shrill ring of the phone interrupted her thoughts, and she stood to answer it, her knees aching as she lifted them one by one from the hard floor.

'Hello?' She tried to massage the life back into them with her free hand.

'You all right? You sound like you're in pain.'

'I'm fine.' Peggy flexed one leg, then the other in an effort to get the blood back to her feet. 'I was kneeling on the floor.'

'Saying your prayers again?' Jerome's voice was mocking. 'I thought we talked about that.'

'No, smart-arse, I was stacking shelves. You know … working. You might have come across the concept.'

'Ah now, baby sister. Only kidding. And amn't I working here too? I am this very moment on my way out to meet a fellah about the television.'

'Yeah?'

'Yes. And a friend of mine happens to know one of the guys this man works with, so we might get a good price on a colour one.'

'Really?' Peggy found she couldn't contain her enthusiasm for this bit of information. She'd been arguing for the installation of a television in the bar for months, but she'd only hoped to get a black and white one, second-hand. This was news.

'Really.'

'Right, so.' They were silent for a moment. 'So why are you phoning?'

'Just checking in.'

The phone went quiet again, but Peggy could hear Jerome's thoughts working up to some sort of request. Her brother wouldn't phone her for nothing.

'Actually, I was wondering if maybe you'd manage okay there tonight? If I were back, say, lunchtime tomorrow? Would that be okay?'

Peggy didn't really mind if Jerome was there to help her that evening. It was unlikely that they'd be busy enough to need a second behind the bar. And anyway, Carla would be back later, so she could help out. But Peggy wanted to make Jerome sweat. Just a little. She saw Maura glance over at her from her perch on one of the benches, her hands hidden under the skirt of a lampshade protruding from the wall. Peggy turned her back on her.

'Peg?'

'You know Friday nights can be busy, Jerome,' she hissed down the phone. 'Last Friday was busy enough. What if a group of fishermen comes in? Or I have to change a keg?'

'Now, when have we last had a big group of anglers?' he asked. 'Sure the water's too low; there are hardly any of them around. Wasn't the competition cancelled? And won't Carla be back? Couldn't she help you?'

Peggy could feel Maura's indignation burning into her back. She didn't want to drag this out any longer than was necessary.

'Go on. You're a useless big brother.'

'And you are a darling little sister. I'll make it up to you.'

'You will,' Peggy said. 'I might decide I fancy a night up in Dublin myself one of these weekends.'

Jerome was quiet for a second. 'Sure thing,' he said at last. 'Look, I'd better go. I'm on a friend's phone.'

'Right so.' Peggy didn't ask any more. She didn't want to know.

'See you tomorrow, Peg.'

Peggy put the receiver down, keeping her back to Maura who had started polishing the tables.

'Weren't you going to mention the news?' Maura asked Peggy, incredulous. 'The body?'

Peggy laughed. 'I never even thought of it,' she said, surprised at herself. 'Ah sure he'll hear about it soon enough. He'll be up in the morning.'

'Huh.' Maura scoured one of the little wooden tables, searching for a shine that had been long since lost. 'You'd think they found bodies every day of the week around here.'

THREE

Almost three hours after leaving Dublin, Frank saw the first sign for Crumm. Not a signpost for the village, but a large, wooden, homemade-looking sign for 'The Angler's Rest, Crumm'. Frank pulled in just ahead of it. Resting his arm on the passenger seat, he looked over his shoulder, let a Morris Minor pass, and reversed back to take a better look. Someone had gone to a lot of trouble over the sign. 'The Angler's Rest, Crumm' it said in stencilled black paint across the top. Beneath, the words 'Casey's Bar' were scripted. A sprightly looking fish leapt up from the bottom left-hand corner, and the words 'Food Served All Day' were diagonally across the right. Frank knew nothing about angling. He had no idea what type of fish was pictured, but he knew he was hungry, and that the chances of two places serving food all day in Crumm were slim. The final pieces of information on the overcrowded sign were an arrow and the words 'turn left after two miles'.

Frank indicated and pulled back out onto the road. He glanced at the clock on the dashboard. Ten to three. He should probably go straight to the station. Garda O'Dowd would be waiting for him. His stomach growled and he regretted not stopping along the way to eat something. With his arm resting on the open window, he concentrated on not missing the turn for Crumm. Although it was the last weekend in September, it might have been mid-August. The sun was lower in the sky, but felt just as strong. The breeze on his bare arm was warm, full of the smell of cut grass and hay. The air smelt different away from the sea. Heavier, sweeter. Frank filled his lungs with it. There were certainly worse places to be on a Friday afternoon, he thought, although the image of Rose thumping him with indignation at the sentiment immediately popped into his head.

He might easily have missed the small sign for the village, were it not for a second billboard beneath it reminding road users of the food served 'All Day' at The Angler's Rest. Frank slowed to make the left turn, and was met by a flood of brown, as a herd of cattle made its way across the road in front of him. The animals spilled from a gate to his left, pushing against each other like drunken ladies in stilettos. They ignored Frank; although he noticed one or two of them skip away at the sight of a nervous-looking dog just ahead of his car. A scarecrow of a man followed the last animal out of the field, stick held aloft in one hand, the other pulling the gate closed behind him. He nodded in Frank's direction. The cattle jostled their way along the road a little before turning right into another field. The farmer followed the last one in, and his dog paced the open gateway like a sentry, as Frank drove slowly past.

The main road from Dublin had been no racetrack, and the Crumm road was worse. Frank winced as his tyres bounced over craters and ruts. Wherever it was given the opportunity, grass did its utmost to reclaim the land stolen by the tarmac. After about a mile, the sound of high-pitched voices broke through the background noises of the countryside. Frank slowed again, and in a clearing to his right, a grey, single-storey building appeared; an alien structure in the blanket of green. Outside, small groups of uniformed teenagers congregated; bags at their feet, jumpers tied around their waists. More walked in pairs and threes through the gate towards the road, chattering, laughing. The sweet freedom of a sunny Friday afternoon in September. Many heads turned

11

or looked up as Frank approached, watching him as he cruised past. One face caught his eye, a tall girl with bushy blonde hair. Her eyes met his, and he gripped the steering wheel a little tighter. Frank knew how it was. There probably weren't many Ford Capris in Crumm, fewer being driven by a twenty-something-year-old bloke with no one in the passenger seat. He could almost hear the hush descend on the yard as he picked up speed and drove away. They'd probably assume he was an angler up from Dublin. Or maybe they had heard about the body and were expecting the Garda. Frank checked his rear-view mirror, but the road was empty. There were certainly worse places to be on a Friday.

Then he sat a little straighter in his seat. This was not some weekend break on the lake. Some poor git was dead, and whether or not the body was ancient, as they suspected, Frank needed to remember why he was there. The third sign for The Angler's Rest was so enormous that he first glimpsed it almost half a mile before he arrived at it. He kept the engine idling at the fork in the road where the sign urged him to turn left down towards the lakeshore and the food, before pulling out and heading right towards the village of Crumm. He had better go straight to the station and put the poor guard out of his misery. The Angler's Rest would have to wait.

FOUR

About the time that Detective Ryan was pulling into the Garda Station in Crumm, Peggy was leaning over the bar at The Angler's Rest, flicking through a magazine; her head propped up on one hand; her long dark locks pooling on the counter over her shoulder. Her other hand, she alternately lifted to her mouth and swept with venom across the colourful pages of tall, thin, tanned girls in short dresses and bell bottoms. Peggy knew that her weekly magazine purchase was a form of subliminal self-torture, but she was afraid to lose her primary contact with the world outside of Crumm. So each Friday lunchtime, she made the pilgrimage to McGowan's General Supplies. She was fairly sure that the magazines had been delivered on Thursdays for weeks now, but that Mrs. McGowan had neglected to inform her in order that she herself might keep up-to-date with the latest styles and make-up trends at Peggy's expense.

Peggy snorted aloud at the sight of a model in a pair of denim dungarees and a cowboy hat. Maybe she should wear a cowboy hat behind the bar. That would give her customers a laugh. They would all think she was losing her mind, when in actuality she would be the only fashionable person in Crumm. She stood up straighter, challenging the model looking back at her. Well at least she herself had good hair. Although it would be better if it were blonde. But the Caseys were all dark. Two girls with hair like thoroughbreds traversed the next double-page spread, clad in turquoise jumpsuits. She swivelled to see her reflection in the mirror running along the back of the bar, bringing the flat of her hand against her face, and flicking back the front of her hair like the girls in the picture. But as soon as she glanced down again at the pages, her hair fell into its usual place. She needed layers. If she had layers, she would be able to flick it out properly. A round brush and a squirt of hairspray would do it. She held back the end of her hair to try and recreate the effect, but dropped it again in resignation. She'd die before asking Mrs. Byrne to cut layers into her hair. As if Mrs. Byrne would even know what that meant. And she shuddered at the idea of bringing the picture with her to the salon. They'd have a great laugh. That Peggy with her big ideas. Food in the bar. Layers in her hair. Whatever next?

Peggy sighed at her reflection; mottled and tarnished in the old mirror. Sure what was the point, anyway? She might have good hair, but her pale skin and rosy cheeks were nowhere to be found on the pages of her magazine. And she'd have to lose two stone to be anywhere near as skinny as those girls. Like Carla. Carla could wear miniskirts and little dresses. Carla had legs like stilts. But she doesn't have my hair, Peggy thought meanly.

She glanced at the clock on the wall. A quarter past three. She would be here soon. Peggy looked back at her own reflection, processing her feelings. Right now, she was looking forward to her sister's arrival. The week was quiet with only Jerome's unpredict-able appearances to bring life to the place. But she knew it wouldn't last. It wouldn't be long before she'd hear Carla's little car pull up outside, and the neighbour's dog would bark, and Carla would bark back at it. She'd come through and into the bar, stooping a little at the archway, and they'd smile at each other. And it would be all downhill from there. No matter how sincere Peggy's sisterly love was for Carla, she knew that by Monday morning there would be no sound more pleasing to her than that of her sister's car pulling away on its early return journey to Wexford.

But then, she also knew that her hard-wired sibling sensibilities would contrive to rebuild an eager anticipation of her sister's return the following Friday. And then Carla would appear, and the cycle would repeat itself. Peggy had long thought that, were she and Carla mere school friends, they would have parted company years ago. They were simply incompatible. And yet, every week, she fooled herself into thinking that things might be different.

The silence of the bar was suddenly broken by the telephone's ring. Just as she reached to answer it, Peggy heard a car on the gravel outside. She looked at the clock again. Carla was early.

'Angler's Rest? Hello?'

'Peggy? Is that you? 'Tis Bernie here.'

'Hello Mrs. O'Shea.' Peggy instinctively pushed the phone closer to her ear. It was unlike Bernie O'Shea to pay for a phone call when she could send Enda over on foot with a message. 'Everything all right?'

'Yes, yes. I will be having Detective Ryan from Dublin staying with me tonight, and I wanted to check that you would be serving food this evening. I can of course prepare something for him here, but it would have to be cold. It's bridge night at the Corcoran's. And who knows what time he will come in from the lake, or whatever it is he will be doing.' Bernie O'Shea's game of bridge was clearly not going to be disrupted, even for a dead body. 'Can I direct him to you? Will you look after him?'

'Of course, Mrs. O'Shea.' Peggy waved at Carla who had stalked into the room, and dropped her bag against the wall. Carla stuck her tongue out at the phone when she heard the name. Her low opinion of Mrs. O'Shea had been honed during the summer of 1970 when she and Enda O'Shea Junior were secretly courting. At least, until such time as Mrs. O'Shea had caught them fumbling in one of her guest bedrooms.

Peggy glared at her sister. 'I'll be sure to feed him, Mrs. O'Shea. Thank you for the referral.'

Carla snorted as she stooped to grab a Coke bottle from the shelf behind her.

Peggy replaced the receiver. 'What?' She looked at Carla. They were already on their slippery slope and she wasn't in the bar thirty seconds.

'Referral?' Carla sniggered, and took a swig from the bottle.

'What about it?' Peggy lifted a clean glass from a shelf and placed it on the counter.

Carla ignored it. She walked around and sat on one of the high stools like a customer. 'Who is she referring to anyway?'

'A guard up from Dublin.' Peggy picked up a cloth and started polishing pint glasses. 'A body was found down by the lake last night.'

Carla's eyes widened. 'You're jokin'!'

'Yeah. Some anglers, pulling in their boat. Apparently they saw it buried at the shore.'

'Jesus.' Carla straightened her neck. 'They saw an actual body?'

'Well, no. I don't know exactly. The waterline's so far back; the lake's lower than it's ever been. I think they saw the outline. Of the body. It might have been a coffin.' Peggy could sense the shock-factor of her news diminishing. 'I'm not really sure.'

Carla's shoulders slumped. 'So it could have been there since the valley was flooded?'

'Maybe. They don't know.'

Carla swigged from the bottle. Peggy noticed her fingernails were painted a deep pink. What was a schoolteacher doing painting her nails midweek? It was a nice colour though.

'Sure it's probably just one of the graves they moved before the dam went up,' Carla said. 'Or rather, one of the graves they should have moved.'

'But the graveyard was on the other side of the valley. Close to where the new one is.'

'Hmm.' Carla considered this. She drained her bottle and handed it to Peggy. 'Sure we might hear more if your referral appears looking for his dinner.'

Exasperated. That's a good word to describe how she makes me feel, thought Peggy, as she slid the Coke bottle into an empty crate on the floor next to her. Carla reached for Peggy's magazine and sat looking at the pages, all the while pushing back her cuticles with a pink talon. Peggy tried to distract herself with thoughts about the Irish stew she had prepared that morning. She would need to get it back into the Aga by four. The phone on the wall rang again.

'Angler's Rest? Hello?' If she had it in by four, it would ready for five. Half past at the latest. 'Hello?' she said again to the silence on the line.

'Eh, hello. Would Miss Cas … eh Carla, be there please?'

Peggy turned to Carla who had lifted her gaze and was questioning her sister with her stare. She shrugged and pointed to the receiver in her hand. 'Who should I say is calling?' She waited. Carla was shaking her head violently. Peggy noticed the colour of her cheeks change. 'Eh, no Tom,' she said. 'Carla hasn't arrived yet, although I am expecting her. I will of course. She has your number?' By now Carla was making angry hang up gestures at her. 'I will of course. Thank you, Tom.' She hung the handset back in its cradle.

'Jesus, I thought you were going to ask after his family,' Carla spat. 'Couldn't you just have said, "she's not here"?'

Indignant. There's another word for how she makes me feel, thought Peggy. 'What's your problem?' she threw back at her. 'Who is Tom anyway?'

Carla looked at her, and retreated. 'No one,' she said.

'Tom.' Peggy wasn't in the humour to give her sister any easy ride. 'Not Tom Devereux? Your school principal?' Carla said nothing. 'Maybe I should have asked after his family.' Peggy couldn't help feeling shocked, and Carla's reddening cheeks were doing little to allay her suspicions. 'He is married, isn't he?'

17

Carla flicked a little too quickly through Peggy's magazine. 'And why are you assuming he wasn't calling about work?' She didn't raise her eyes from the pages.

Peggy reached out and rubbed her thumb over one of Carla's painted nails. 'I assumed you would take the call if it was just about work,' she said. Carla pulled her hand away. Peggy drew the cloth from her shoulder and resumed polishing the glasses.

'I'm not judging,' she said, after some moments of silence.

'Good,' Carla replied, hopping off the stool and picking up her bag from the floor. She stood for a second, fiddling with the strap. 'Thank you.' The words were barely audible. She made her way towards a door in the back of the bar, leading to the main house. 'I'm going inside,' she said.

'I'll need you later,' Peggy said. 'Jerome's staying in Dublin tonight.' She waited for a tirade of complaints and bitching about her and her brother's inability to manage the family business. It didn't come.

'Okay,' Carla said. 'That's another Casey on a shady road to iniquity.' Peggy looked up from her work to see if Carla's face betrayed her true meaning, but all she saw was her sister's back as she disappeared into the house.

FIVE

From the moment Garda O'Dowd tucked his long limbs into Frank's car, he seemed to forget all about the body at the lake, and focus only on the Capri's interior; staring in unabashed awe at the dashboard; tracing his fingers along the radio casing, only lifting his gaze once or twice to give Frank directions as they drove from the station towards the lake. When the boreen they were on finally came to an abrupt dead end, Garda O'Dowd seemed to remember what he was supposed to be doing, and pointed out Frank's side window.

'There. You can pull in there.'

Frank drove slowly into a clearing, where grass was trying but largely failing in its effort to push through the sun-baked ground. With the engine off, they sat in eerie silence, staring out over the lake. They had stopped in what seemed to be a makeshift car park, where fishermen could conveniently leave their cars and trailers while they went off on the water. It was really just a small field, edged by tall evergreens to the back, and opening out to the lake at the front. Parked as they were, facing the lake, Frank could see how low the water level was. A person could easily walk twenty yards from the edge of the clearing before their feet would get wet, and it was apparent from the barrenness of the grey sand that those twenty yards were unaccustomed to being exposed to the air.

Frank got out of the car and walked to the edge of the grass where the clearing met the lakeshore proper. A small drop, less than a foot in places, showed where the lake's water habitually lapped. Now, Frank could step down onto the silty soil, littered with small rocks and pebbles, and walk on the lakebed with ease.

Garda O'Dowd followed him. 'It's just over here.' He pointed past Frank to his right. 'A little way along. I left one of the O'Malley lads at the site.' He glanced up at Frank with apparent unease. 'I was reluctant to leave it unguarded. Not that I'd expect any interference. But you never know.'

Frank said nothing, but walked in the direction the younger guard had indicated. He looked around him as he went, taking in the lake, the shoreline, the somehow unnatural layout of it all. He felt the ground beneath his feet soften as they ventured further. Garda O'Dowd hurried ahead, his hand up, shielding his eyes from the afternoon sun. Wetness oozed around Frank's leather shoes as they got closer to the water's edge. The shoreline jutted out a little just ahead of them, and the trunks of tall evergreens blocked the view somewhat; their long needles swinging and swishing high above. Frank began to feel the dampness in his feet, and was considering taking his shoes and socks off when he noticed a lad of no more than eighteen walking towards them. Garda O'Dowd spoke quietly to him, and the lad nodded his tight red curls in earnest, and pointed to a spot only yards from where they stood.

Garda O'Dowd turned to Frank. 'It's just here, Detective Sergeant.'

Unlike a sandy seaside beach, the silty ground between the water's edge and the natural shoreline was grey and flat. The stones that littered the area closer to the shore were absent further out, and the area of ground Garda O'Dowd gestured towards seemed to Frank to be an unvarying expanse of plain, drying mud. But as they got closer, Frank could see that one part of the ground, a strip of about five feet by two, was a darker grey than the rest, and that the silt around this shape was uneven, sagging in places, and rounding at the edges.

Despite the heat, Frank shivered. He looked up at the two men, only to see them looking back at him expectantly. Frank acknowledged the young lad with a nod.

'Sir,' the lad said.

'You haven't disturbed it at all?'

'No, sir.' The lad looked from one officer to the other. They were still ten feet from the ominous shape on the ground, but all seemed to share an apparent reluctance to encroach any further.

''Twas two fishermen found it, Detective Sergeant.' Garda O'Dowd took a small notebook from his trouser pocket and flipped over a few pages before settling on one filled with scribbled notes. 'Late last evening. A John Forkin and a Thomas O'Reilly. They're not locals, but they say that they would return should we need to speak with them again.'

Frank looked up at the young guard.

'I did interview them, of course,' he continued, glancing quickly at the young red-headed boy who was still standing close by. 'Last night, here, at the scene. One of them, eh,' he consulted his notes, 'Thomas O'Reilly. He went on up to the Hanleys' up the way.' He gestured with his notebook up along the road they had just driven down. 'And I was summoned. And I came down here.' He wiped the back of his hand across his brow. 'To the scene of the crime, as it were.'

Frank looked down at the shape under the sand. 'Well, we don't know if it is a crime yet, of course,' he said. He knew he was teasing, but it was difficult not to. The young officer invited ridicule with his baby face and his nervous manner.

'Of course, sir. Of course.' Garda O'Dowd flushed red. 'Some of the locals suggested that it might be an old grave. From before the dam.'

'This whole valley was flooded,' the boy spoke suddenly, his eyes wide, his arms outstretched across the lake. 'There was a whole

21

village here once, sir, before they built the dam. The whole thing was drown'ded. Out there.' He pointed out to the middle of the lake.

Frank followed his gaze. He could just make out some sort of stone, or rock, protruding from the still water.

'The water's so low now you can see the tops of them buildin's, sir. Although most were blasted down, they say. But some were left.'

'Yes, thank you, Cormac,' Garda O'Dowd glared at the boy. He took a handkerchief from his other trouser pocket and mopped the perspiration from his brow again. He turned back to Frank. 'It is possible of course, sir,' he said. 'The main graveyard over at the old manor estate was moved at the time, plot by plot, to a site higher up Slieve Mart. But that's over the other side of the village.' He tipped his head back towards the spot Cormac had been pointing to. 'So it couldn't be one of those. Coleman thinks it must be from another time altogether.'

'Coleman?' Frank started to step tentatively towards the shape in the ground.

'He'd be the eldest around here,' Cormac saw fit to interject again before being hushed by another glare from Garda O'Dowd.

'He's lived here all his life,' Garda O'Dowd said to Frank. 'Since before the flooding even. He'd be, oh, certainly in his seventies.' He raised his eyebrows at Cormac who nodded in agreement.

'The local sage,' Frank said to himself. He stood as close to the shape as he could, and crouched down until his face was only a couple of feet from whatever it was that was buried there. The sand was smooth, except for the end closest to the shore, where it appeared disturbed, and Frank could see some type of cloth sticking out of the silt.

'Ah, that is where I investigated last evening, sir,' Garda O'Dowd said from his standing point five feet off. 'The shape of the mound was, of course, suggestive of a grave, or, eh, a body,' he coughed. 'But I felt the need to be sure, sir, before I alerted the Superintendent. I didn't want to be causing a commotion for a, eh, false alarm, sir.'

Frank didn't answer. He leaned in as close to the exposed material as he could without falling onto the sand himself. It was coarse, like flax or some other type of sacking. It was certainly somewhat degraded. Definitely not new. He reached down and lifted the raw edge a little. Without turning, he could sense the trepidation of his two companions.

'It's just beneath the sacking, sir.' Garda O'Dowd swallowed loudly. 'You can, I think, see some, eh, remains.'

Sure enough, Frank could make out what seemed to him to be matted, black hair. Human hair. He dropped the cloth and stood up straight, wiping his hand roughly on his jeans.

A moment of silence passed between them. Cormac O'Malley blessed himself quickly three times, the reality of what he had been guarding only apparently dawning on him at that second.

Frank collected himself. 'You were right to call it in, Garda O'Dowd,' he said at last.

The younger man flushed, nodding in vindication. Frank stared down at the pitiful strip of mounded sand. What poor unfortunate had ended up here? He was fairly sure it was an old grave, but not old enough, he guessed, that it predated a coffin burial. Whoever it was, they had been buried in a sack, and that was no fitting end for any of God's creatures. He ran his hand through his hair, damp from the heat of the afternoon.

'You'll stay here a while longer, Cormac?' He looked at the boy, who nodded, clearly delighted to be considered worthy of assisting a Detective Sergeant all the way from Dublin.

'Sir,' was all he said.

Frank looked at Garda O'Dowd. 'We'll go up to the station, Michael,' he said. 'I'll need to call the pathologist, and update him on the situation. And you, Michael,' he lowered his gaze back to where the tiniest glimpse of black hair was visible in the ground, 'you might go and bring the priest.'

SIX

The bar was a little busier than usual that evening. Although the local angling club's competition had been cancelled due to the low water level in the lake, some of the more committed fishermen had decided to make the journey anyway. Since five o'clock, Peggy had already fed two groups of three, when another two strangers walked in through the door of the pub in sleeveless poacher jackets and bucket hats. They sat up at the bar, and one of them ordered two pints of Guinness. Peggy half filled two glasses and left them to settle.

'Would ye like to see the menu?' she asked.

'Ara, no thanks love.' The older of the two looked at his companion. 'I'll have to make tracks after this one. I told herself I'd be back for the dinner.'

Peggy nodded, and finished pulling the two pints. She thought of how busy the weekend could have been. Sometimes a hundred people attended the last competition of the season. They wouldn't all have eaten in the pub, of course, but it could have been a really lucrative weekend, nonetheless. Even in the days before they had started serving food, the Casey teenagers would have been expected to hang around on competition weekends in case they were needed in the bar.

She put the two pints in front of the men and took the money handed to her. It would have been around this time of year when she had first been asked to help out herself. A rite of passage in their household, she still remembered the day clearly. She had been sitting outside under the big tree, reading *Little Women*, when her father's bald head had appeared at the door of the pub. He had asked her to collect the empty glasses that had been abandoned on the wooden bench outside. After leaving them on the bar, she had stayed, listening to the fishermen talk as they stood drinking pints, hiding behind them so her father wouldn't see her.

But after a while, she had realized that her father was too busy with customers to notice her at all, and she had started to clear empties from tables inside the pub too. She'd watched Carla, probably only fifteen at the time, flirting with strange men from Dublin as she wiped spills and stacked used pint glasses in the crook of her arm. Carla had been tall even back then. She could easily have passed for seventeen, or even eighteen. Hugo and Jerome had been behind the bar with her father. Peggy closed her eyes for a moment, trying to see her mother in the picture. She turned back to the two anglers who were ogling their untouched pints. She handed the older one his change. Where had her mother been that day? And then she remembered, and she could see her sitting in the back kitchen next to the Aga, her face pale with pain, her hands thin and anxious, her smile bright as she saw Peggy come in from the bar to make her a cup of tea.

That had been the first day she had worked for her father in the bar, but not the last. Who would have thought, that of the four of them, it would be Peggy working here alone now most days? Not for the first time, she tried to imagine her father's reaction to the situation. He would certainly have been surprised. He would have expected Peggy to be working in one of the hotels in Galway or Dublin by now, maybe even assistant manager of one of the smaller ones. That had been the plan. But then isn't that the way with plans? They have a tendency not to pan out as expected. And he would have been disappointed in Jerome and Hugo, that was for sure. Especially Hugo. Peggy thought about her eldest brother, away in London, working at God only knows what. He had been expected to take over the family business, like a million eldest sons before him. Their father had expected it, their mother had expected it, the whole village had expected it. Peggy herself had taken it as a fact of life. When her father needed him to, Hugo would come back from London, or wherever he might have been, and pick up where Patrick Casey had left off. It was generally assumed that Mr. Casey had died of a broken heart. But Peggy was of the opinion that the shock of Hugo's refusal to stay on in Crumm after their mother's funeral did more damage to their father.

'Another round? Miss? Are you with us?'

Before Peggy could react, a voice from behind her said, 'three pints? I'll drop them down,' and Carla materialized out of nowhere. 'What's wrong with you?' She took three pint glasses from the shelf and tilted one under the tap. 'Are you asleep? It's not Waterford crystal you know.' She nodded at the tumbler Peggy was polishing with a cloth.

Peggy looked at the glass and put it down on the shelf. 'Where did you come out of?'

'I was just checking to see if you needed any help.' Carla started on the third pint. 'I can stay here for a while if you like. Do you want to get some dinner in the back?'

'No. No thanks.' Peggy stood up and flexed her shoulders. 'I'm grand here.' She walked out from behind the bar and went to collect empty plates from a table where three men were sitting.

One of them smiled up at her. 'That was lovely now, thanks girl,' he said, his ruddy cheeks and crackled nose telling of many seasons on the lake. 'Did you make it yourself?'

'I did.' Peggy smiled back.

'Beautiful, beautiful.' One of the other two men at the table lifted his hand in thanks, his eyes never leaving the pint glass in front of him, his grey beard bouncing against his collar.

'Could ye be tempted to a slice of homemade apple tart with cream?' Peggy asked.

'Oh Lord,' the affable, red-faced man patted his ample stomach. 'I'm sure we shouldn't but if it's as good as the stew, sure we'd better give it a go.' He nodded at the other two who seemed happy to go along with whatever their companion decided.

Peggy smiled at him and took the plates behind the bar. 'I'll just be a sec,' she told Carla, and went in through the door to the kitchen.

Five minutes later, she walked back into the bar carrying three plates of warm apple tart; a little cloud of cream melting on each one. She sensed immediately that the bar was fuller, and noticed a new table of three men, younger than the usual fishermen, the three of them watching Carla as she placed their pints before them. She put the plates of apple tart down to appreciative grunts and gentle chants of 'beautiful, beautiful,' from the bearded man. Back behind the bar, when she looked up, there was a man sitting right at the end of the counter on a high stool.

'Oh, sorry,' she smiled. 'I didn't see you there. What can I get you?'

The man looked amused. 'Have I stumbled onto some Amazonian public house?'

'I beg your pardon?' Peggy looked directly at him.

He glanced over at Carla. 'It's not often you come across bars being run only by women,' he said.

'Who's to say I haven't got a big lump of a man out the back?' Peggy cocked her head towards the back door.

The man laughed, but then seemed to collect himself. He sat up straighter on the stool. 'I'm sure you have no need of one,' he said. 'I'll have a pint, so.'

Peggy put a glass to the tap. He was a funny one. It wasn't too often they got strangers on their own in Crumm. Even the anglers tended to come in little groups after a day on the lake. You might get the odd German passing through, but Peggy knew this fellah was no more German than she was herself. His accent was soft.

A monied lilt. First generation Dublin, she guessed. Carla handed her some used glasses over the bar, winking at her. Peggy scowled back. She noticed the stranger stealing a glance at them both.

'So,' she said, topping up the pint, 'are you here for the fishing?'

'Not exactly.' He put some coins down on the counter. He drew the pint over to him, and lifted it to his lips. 'Sláinte,' he said, and sucked back a third of it before it had a proper chance to settle.

Peggy could see tables that needed clearing, but she stayed where she was behind the counter, rinsing glasses that had already been rinsed.

'So is this your place?' he said at last.

'It is,' Peggy replied. 'Well, mine and my siblings. It's a family business.'

He nodded. Peggy watched him stroke the pint glass. She wondered if he might be one of the contractors in to help a local farmer make the last of the hay. His fingers were long and tanned. His fingernails were clean. She dragged his coins across the bar with the flat of her palm, catching his eye as she did so. Facing the till, she could see his reflection as he took another drink from his glass.

'So if you're not a fisher, and you're not a farmer, what is it that you do?' She spoke to his reflection as she slowly tidied the till drawer.

'What makes you think I'm not a farmer?' His mouth curled in a smile.

Peggy turned and leaned heavily against the drawer, closing it. She nodded at his glass. 'They're not the fingers of a manual labourer,' she said.

Frank regarded his hand, turning it front to back.

'No?'

'No.'

'So I'm too clean to be a farmer?'

She smiled despite herself. 'Something like that,' she said.

They were still looking at each other, when Carla came around the bar, dirty pint glasses dangling from each hand.

She ignored Peggy and smiled openly at the man sitting at the bar as she left the glasses on the counter. He glanced from one sister to the other.

'Hello,' he said.

'Hello.' Carla smiled back. Peggy rolled her eyes and turned back to the till. Carla stuck her hand across the bar at him. 'Carla Casey.'

'Eh, Frank Ryan,' he said. 'Detective Sergeant Frank Ryan.'

Carla's kohl-streaked eyes were suddenly wide and she slapped her hands down on the bar. 'Oh, are you up from Dublin for the body?' She seemed to have forgotten about Peggy, who was standing behind her, watching Frank in the mirror. 'So tell us, is it just one of the ones from the old graveyard?' She leant on the bar opposite Frank and rested her chin in her hand. 'Or was it new? Do you know who it is?'

'Eh, well, I'm not really at liberty to discuss it right now.' Frank sat back a little on his stool. 'The pathologist will be here tomorrow. He'll have to examine the body.'

'So there definitely is a body?' Carla asked him. 'It wasn't just some old, empty box left there? You actually found a body?'

'Eh, yes.' Frank looked from Carla to Peggy's reflection and back. 'There was a body. There is a body. It does appear to be old though.' He coughed. 'As in, of course we can't be sure until the pathologist examines it, but it would appear to be, eh, old.'

'Oh.' Carla straightened up again. 'Ah well.' She lifted a cloth from the sink and wrung it out. 'Well,' she said, 'it's a pleasure to meet you, Detective Ryan. Peggy here will look after you. I'm sure you must be famished having travelled all the way from Dublin. Peggy,' she stared, wide-eyed at her sister. 'Detective Ryan needs a pint.' She tipped her brow to the glass of dregs still gripped in Frank's hand, and turned to wipe down the counter with the cloth.

Peggy drew a calming breath and looked at Frank. 'So, Detective,' she said.

'Frank.'

'Frank. Another pint, Frank?'

'Well, actually, if you are serving food … ' Frank glanced around at the empty plates Carla was now clearing from a table behind him.

'Oh Lord, of course,' Peggy clasped her hand to her mouth. 'Mrs. O'Shea told me to expect you. That you would need feeding.'

'I think she had a prior appointment for this evening.'

'Bridge night,' Peggy nodded. 'Even a Detective Sergeant from Dublin doesn't come before bridge night, I'm afraid.'

Frank smiled. 'Well, her husband offered to make me a sandwich,' he said. 'I think that was all he was getting himself.'

'Poor Enda,' Peggy smiled at Frank. 'Well we can certainly feed you, Frank. If you like stew?'

'Stew would be lovely, thank you. And I will.' He tilted the glass in his hand.

'You will?'

'Have another.'

Just at that moment, the main door opened, and Peggy looked up to see Garda O'Dowd entering the bar. Even after he removed his cap, he had to stoop so as not to hit his head on the lintel. He glanced around the place, nodding at familiar faces, before approaching the counter. Carla pushed past him, her arms laden with dirty plates and cutlery.

'Carla. Peggy,' he said, tipping his head at the two women behind the bar, fidgeting with the cap in his hands all the while. 'Detective Sergeant,' he said looking at Frank.

'Michael.'

Peggy noticed the beads of sweat on Garda O'Dowd's brow as she pulled Frank's pint. She tried not to notice the smell of sweat that the young guard seemed to have brought in with him. The perils of a young man left in charge of his own laundry, she thought to herself. He stood there, looking from one sister to the other, nervously passing the cap back and forth through his fingers. He seemed to be waiting for Frank to say something. Peggy could sense her sister's exasperation rising.

'Big day at the office for you, Michael,' Carla said. Michael blushed madly as he looked from her to Frank.

'Indeed,' he said.

'Oh, they'll be looking for you over in New York after this, I'd say,' Carla stood with the plates still in her arms. 'I'd say the FBI will be looking to poach you. Don't ye think?' She elbowed Peggy, who stayed silent.

Michael just flicked his eyes at her again, before addressing Frank. 'Sir? Eh, maybe we could, eh, talk a moment?' He gestured with his cap across to a quiet corner of the room where there was a small table with two stubby stools either side of it.

Frank looked over at it. 'Of course.' He lifted his pint and stood to go. Then he stopped and pushed his free hand deep into the pocket of his jeans.

'No, no,' Peggy said. 'I'll get you your meal first. We can sort it out after.'

Frank nodded at her.

'Will you be eating, Garda O'Dowd?' she looked at Michael.

He shook his head. 'No, no, Peggy. Thank you.'

'Right. Well, why don't you gentlemen sit over there, and I'll be right out with your meal, Frank.'

Peggy noticed Michael's eyebrows arch at her familiarity. She smiled to herself. Let him think her forward. She left Carla in the bar and went to plate out some stew for Frank. She'd put it on one of her mother's Aynsley dinner plates. They looked nicer than the everyday ones.

Peggy hummed to herself as she stirred the pot on the Aga, looking for some good-sized pieces of meat. It wasn't often there were interesting strangers in The Angler's Rest. And she couldn't help feeling that this weekend was going to be a little more interesting than usual.

SEVEN

Despite the warmth of the day, autumn could not be denied. The evening light had all but faded by the time most of the fishermen had gone home, and the local regulars had taken up their usual places in Casey's. The old sash windows were still open, and the cooler air mixed with the smell of smoke and kegs and the stew; a comforting smell of home for Peggy. They would normally have a fire lit at this time of year, she thought, looking at the blackened grate that hadn't seen a spark for what must be four months now. It had been such a summer; they just hadn't needed it. She might light one tomorrow night. It would be nice to have it lit.

'You should have lit the fire.' Carla's teacher-like intonation assailed Peggy's ears. Her sister stood behind her, sorting coins in the opened till drawer. 'It gives the place a bit of life.' She shivered. 'And God knows it could do with a bit of life.'

Peggy heard it slam shut. She decided to ignore her sister.

'Although,' Carla elbowed her in the ribs, 'yer man over there,' she tipped her head towards Frank, who was sitting with an empty dessert plate before him, a newspaper in one hand, and a mug of coffee in the other, 'he's a bit of life. No?' She elbowed Peggy again.

Before Peggy could retort, the door opened, and a diminutive elderly man walked into the bar.

'Oh, Jaysus, well here's the walking dead,' Carla said under her breath, and went off around the bar to clear Frank's table.

The man walked in slowly through the porch, his eyes only leaving the flagstone floor briefly to acknowledge two younger men seated with pints at a low table. He was dressed for colder weather, wearing an old tweed jacket over a wool shirt and threadbare jumper. His trousers were two sizes too big, gathered in at the waist by a length of rope. Strands of white hair poked out from under his plaid cap, which he removed and hung on a hook next to the fireplace.

'Young wan,' he nodded to Peggy as he approached the bar.

'Coleman,' she said. 'It's getting cooler at last out there now, I think.'

''Tis that, child. 'Tis that.' Coleman sat up on a stool and crossed his arms. Peggy pulled him a pint, and he watched the contents of the glass settle. After a moment, she filled it and placed it on the bar in front of him. He sat up straighter, and rubbed the white stubble on his chin, regarding the pint as if it was something he had never seen in his life before. Then he lifted it and drank some back, stealing a glance to his right as he did, to where Frank was seated with his paper. Peggy watched his ritual. She noticed how his white hair curled like a baby's around his ears. He could do with a visit to Mrs. Byrne's himself, she thought. The idea made her smile. She knew it was more likely that he'd get his brother to cut any stray locks with a kitchen knife.

'That's a fine pint.' He nodded at Peggy, wiping the froth from his whiskers. 'A fine pint.'

'Oh, only the best at Casey's,' Peggy sighed, lifting a bottle of fizzy orange from the shelf behind her. She opened it and poured it into a glass for herself, popping a plastic straw in from a box beside the till. She could drink it more discreetly from a straw. Carla was sitting with a few local lads, soaking up their unbridled admiration. So much for her helping out. Peggy noticed Coleman take another sideways glance at Frank who was standing up to leave. Frank removed his wallet from his back pocket and took out a note. She couldn't help but notice the strawberry blond hairs on his chest just below his neck, where the top two buttons of his shirt were left open.

'Thank you for that,' he said to her, leaving the note down on the counter between them. 'It was very nice.'

'You're very welcome.' Peggy took the note and turned quickly to the till to hide her reddening cheeks. She glanced up into the mirror. Frank was standing awkwardly next to Coleman, the older man pointedly ignoring him as he gazed down into his pint.

'Frank, have you met Coleman?' Peggy said loudly into the till. She turned and handed Frank his change. 'Coleman has lived in Crumm all his life. He knows more about the area than anyone. Coleman,' Peggy said, 'this is Detective Sergeant Frank … ' she stopped.

'Ryan,' Frank finished.

'Sorry,' Peggy said. 'Detective Sergeant Frank Ryan. He's down from Dublin because of the body found at the lake. He's been helping Garda O'Dowd with the … the situation.'

Peggy waited. Coleman just nodded slowly at his pint, not looking up at either of them.

'Coleman,' Frank said.

The older man just nodded again.

Peggy threw her eyes to heaven. 'Maybe you might be able to help the guards with their enquiries, Coleman?' She spoke slowly, as if Coleman might not understand. 'You having all the local knowledge. About the valley and the lake.'

Still the older man said nothing.

'He's not from Dublin, Coleman,' Peggy said under her breath. She silently implored Frank not to contradict her. 'He's just stationed there.'

'Is that right?' the older man said at last, from a mouth that was clearly short a few teeth. 'And what part of the world do you hail from, Detective Sergeant?'

'Galway, sir.' Frank winked at Peggy, who was slowly wiping the already clean counter beside them. 'I grew up in Galway. My parents are both from Connemara.'

'I see.' Coleman took a draught of his pint.

'I've lived in Dublin for the past ten years though,' Frank said, a note of defiance in his tone. 'Longer.'

'I suppose you have a ticket for the match Sunday, so,' Coleman said.

Frank thought about the coveted All-Ireland football final ticket he had back in his room in Dublin, wedged in the frame of a picture of Saint Michael his mother had given him. He had a bad feeling that was as close to the Hogan Stand as the ticket was going to get.

'I do', he said.

Coleman drained his pint and left it down on the bar, just a fraction farther away from him than before. Without saying a word, Peggy took the glass away, and began to pull another for him.

'Well,' he said, rubbing his gnarled hands up and down his thighs as if he was trying to massage some life into his legs, 'at least those bastards from Cork aren't going to be there.'

Peggy snorted. 'Oh, if there's one thing we like less than people from Dublin around here, it's people from Cork,' she laughed, shaking her head at Frank.

Frank just smiled, and sat back up on the stool he had occupied earlier that evening. 'So you know the area well,' he said to Coleman. 'Do you remember them moving the graves before the dam was built?'

Coleman looked up at Frank as if he might be mad. 'Sure wasn't it I myself who was doing the moving?' he said, turning back to nod at the fresh pint that Peggy had placed in front of him. He shook his head. 'It was a terrible job, so it was. Upset a lot of people, as you might understand.' He spoke slowly, deliberately; each word pronounced as if it was not his first language he was using.

'I'll get that.' Frank nodded at the glass of stout. 'And I'll have one myself.' He handed Peggy back some of the coins.

The old man's lips twitched and he bobbed his head in Frank's direction. 'A terrible job. But sure, that was what they made us do. They came down from Dublin one day. A group of them. Like Cromwell did before them. Oh, with their measuring instruments, and big cars, and cameras. They took one look at the place and decided the whole lot of it would be better off under water.'

Frank could sense Peggy's embarrassment at the old man's bitter appraisal of the engineers and civil servants who had probably only been doing their job. He guessed Coleman regarded Frank himself in much the same light.

'1946 it was. Not long after the war.' Coleman sat even straighter on his stool, squinting out before him into the past, remembering. For someone who would hardly speak five minutes before, it seemed that he had plenty to say after all. 'But there were shortages of all sorts at that time. It took until 1952 before they finished it. 1948,' he announced loudly, drawing out the words as though they should be set to music. Frank noticed a few of the locals in the bar look over briefly in their direction. '1948, 49. They bought up all the land, from Crumm and Ballyknock on the east of the valley to Slieve Mart on the west. And we all had to get out. That was it. We had the year to leave, that was all.' He turned to Frank and looked him in the eye for the first time in the whole conversation. 'And they did not pay what they should have for that land,' he almost shouted, his eyes blaming Frank. 'That they did not.'

He turned back to his pint and went quiet for a moment. Peggy served another customer at the bar, but Frank could feel her watching them all the while.

'They paid us what they wanted to, and that was that,' Coleman said. 'And we took it, of course.' His voice, quieter now, was tempered with resignation. 'That dam was to be built whether we got a fair price for our land or not. The water would be the sheriff.' His face creased with the memory.

Peggy laid a cardboard coaster on the counter in front of Frank, and set his pint down on it. 'Coleman worked with the other men to move the graves to the new graveyard,' she explained to Frank, looking hopefully at Coleman. 'He might be able to show you where that was. Isn't that right, Coleman?'

Coleman nodded. 'It is,' he said.

He leaned over to one side suddenly. Frank went to catch him, then realized that the man was just reaching into his trouser pocket. He took out a crushed packet of cigarettes and threw them onto the shiny, lacquered bar.

'My land was to be flooded. I'd sold the few cattle I had. There was work to be had at the graveyard for a few of us, so that is what I spent the summer of 1950 doing. Moving bodies.'

He went quiet then. Frank sensed the gravity of what Coleman was describing to him. Even Peggy was silent, as she stood behind the bar opposite where they sat, her arms folded, her eyes fixed on the old man's face.

'That must have been a difficult job,' Frank said.

'Aye. 'Tis better to leave those who are dead in their resting place. No old bones want to be lifted.' He took a cigarette from the box and tapped it on the counter. 'And my own people were there, of course. 'Twas that way for all the men. And if your own people were to be disturbed, you were not to work that day. That was how it was settled.'

Frank shook his head. He couldn't contemplate digging up the bones of the dead, and moving them to be buried somewhere else. It seemed wrong. But then, so did purposely flooding a whole village, and yet that was what had to be done. People wanted electricity, so people had to pay for it. One way or the other. His mind went back to the grave he had stood over earlier that afternoon.

'But the cemetery wasn't near this place? I believe it was across the valley?'

'That's right.' Coleman leaned in over the counter as Peggy struck a match for him. ''Twas across under the shadow of Slieve Mart. Near the manor house. That was where we moved them from. The new cemetery isn't far from the original site. Half a mile further up the hill, no more.'

Frank watched as the man pulled hard on his cigarette. It was clear that the body they had found was not from the old grave-yard. He wasn't really surprised. The shallow depth of the site, and the ominous sacking that the body seemed to be buried in had suggested that it was no consecrated grave. He wanted to ask Coleman outright if he had any idea who it might be, buried there on the shore, being watched over this very night by that young, eager, local lad. Surely if anyone had gone missing from the place in the past few decades, Coleman would know about it. But it was clear to Frank that Coleman didn't trust him. The man's memory of what officials from Dublin could do to a place like Crumm was obviously still fresh.

'So it was a farm you had in the valley?' he asked. 'Was it cattle you said?' He took a slow swig from his pint. He had better pace himself. He suspected that he was going to be in Casey's a little later than he had intended.

Coleman looked as if he were deciding whether to answer Frank or not. After a moment, he spoke. ''Twas my father's land. And his father's before him. And then mine and Desmond's. Ours alone. And we farmed it together.'

'Desmond is Coleman's brother,' Peggy said quickly to Frank.

'They came with the army. After everyone had left. In '51 I think it was. They came with their explosives and they blew the lot up.'

Frank looked up from his pint. 'They blew it up?' he said. 'Your house?'

'Our home … place, the Kilty Bridge, the old mill. Some other buildings in the village. They blew them up. Thought it was a great sport. They clapped each other on the back and took photos for the paper.' Coleman pursed his lips. 'We watched from the bleachers. Those of us who were still around.'

'Did many leave altogether?' Peggy asked. Frank glanced at her but her eyes were fixed on the old man's face.

Coleman looked up at her with a furrowed brow and flicked his cigarette into a big ceramic ashtray she had left down on the bar near to him. 'Hardly a soul stayed,' he said at last. 'The land was gone. There was nothing to stay for.' He fell silent for a moment, his eyes trained on the ashtray. 'Most went up to Dublin. A few of the older ones moved in with family in Crumm. Tom Clancy,' he looked up at Peggy who nodded. 'Tom moved in with his daughter and her family in Ballyknock, Lord have mercy on him.'

A punter gestured to Peggy from across the room and she acknowledged him and reached for a bottle of stout.

'Coleman worked as a postman in the village,' she said to Frank as she flicked the cap off and tilted the bottle into a glass, 'until he retired a few years back.'

More than a few, Frank thought to himself, trying to picture the old man cycling the roads with his bag of letters. But he couldn't help but be struck by the man's story. He had sensed it, down at the lake. Aside from the finding of the body, there was an eeriness about the place. Echoes of bitterness and loss were in the wind that blew up from the water. As he watched Peggy take the bottle and glass over to a man seated by a window, he tried to imagine Coleman and his brother, watching from a distance, as their home was legally blown up before them. Bachelor brothers, probably in their forties at the time, and all they owned in life taken from them without their consent. Too young to retire, too old to move up to Dublin and start anew. It couldn't have been easy. Then he thought of something.

'But I thought I saw the top of a building in the distance today? Out in the middle of the lake?' he said.

'You might well have, the water is so low.' Coleman pushed another empty glass away from him across the bar. 'Part of the mill remains. It didn't all fall like they had wanted it to.' He slapped his hand down on the counter and brandished his tooth-less grin at Frank. 'Them army boys didn't have it all their own way, Detective Sergeant.'

Peggy came back behind the bar, empty pint glasses in her arms. 'Now, now, Coleman', she said, glancing up at Frank, 'there's no need to frighten the customers. You need a drink, I see.'

She went to refill his glass, while the old man sat back into himself, growling something about not being made into a sheep farmer by any army hoor. Frank was thinking of how best to approach the subject of the body with him, when the phone rang loudly on the wall. Peggy turned to answer it, and Coleman eased himself off his high stool and shuffled off towards a door that led out the back to the toilet. Peggy turned in towards the wall and covered her ear with her hand.

'Hello? Casey's?' The line crackled. She could tell someone was there, but the connection was so poor, she couldn't make out what they were saying. 'Hello?' The static stopped, and her ear was assaulted by a man's voice, booming through the receiver.

'I know she's there. Hello? Just let me speak to her. Please. I know she's ... ' The last part of the man's plea was drowned out by a particularly loud burst of static and Peggy put some distance between her ear and the handset. Something made her notice Carla, who was still sitting with her three admirers, but who was staring at Peggy with an accusing look on her face. Peggy tentatively brought the phone back to her ear.

'Hello?'

'Just let me talk to her. Please. Just for a minute.'

The man's speech was slurred, as if he were crying, or drunk, or possibly both. But the line was clearer and Peggy recognized Tom Devereaux's voice, pleading. She glanced back up at Carla, who was stalking across the room towards her, eyes burning. The handset was snatched from her hand and she was met with the back of Carla's head. She hesitated for a moment, before moving away from her sister, and back behind the bar. Coleman had returned and was hoisting himself back up onto his stool.

'You're drunk.' Carla spat the words into the receiver; her head bowed low, her back to the bar. Peggy hovered, moving glasses unnecessarily around on a shelf beneath the bar. She caught Frank's eye, but his face was expressionless.

'You're full of shite, Tom.' The tirade continued behind her. 'Off home with you now. I'm sure she'll have your dinner waiting.'

Peggy wasn't shocked at her sister's tone exactly, more at the fact that some other person could be on the receiving end of it. She'd assumed that Carla only spoke to her siblings like that. She almost pitied Tom Devereaux. He might be an adulterous ass, but she couldn't wish Carla's ire on anyone. She looked at Frank who seemed to be concentrating on looking disinterested. Coleman was busy muttering nothing good into his pint glass.

'Don't you dare Tom.' Carla's voice was getting louder. Peggy looked anxiously around the room, but no one seemed to be taking any heed of her.

'It's bad enough I'll have to look at you on Monday morning. Go to bed. Sleep it off. With your wife.'

The handset was slammed up against the phone and Carla stood staring at it for a moment. Suddenly, she swung around and glared at Peggy, her eyes blazing.

'What?' she spat at her. 'What are you looking at?' Then she seemed to notice Frank watching her, and she turned and walked through the door leading to the house. Peggy watched her go. She considered following her for a second, but quickly decided against it. Turning back to the bar, she looked at Frank.

'That's Carla. She's the quiet, reserved one.'

Frank smiled at her. 'So how many of you are there?'

'Four.' Peggy lifted a mineral glass from the little draining board next to the sink under the bar and started to polish it dry. 'Two brothers, Carla, and me.' She smiled. 'I'm the baby.'

'I see.' Frank twisted his pint glass on the bar. Peggy noticed his eyelashes. They were long and fair. Not blond, but fair. Funny, she thought. She'd never noticed any man's eyelashes before.

'So you and Carla run the place?'

Peggy jumped as the eyelashes suddenly flicked upwards and Frank was looking straight at her again.

'Eh, no. Well, yes. Well, she helps.' Peggy put the glass down and lifted another. 'She helps out. At the weekends. She's a school-teacher,' she said. Frank just nodded. 'It's really me and Jerome. Who run the bar. My brother. He's here most of the time. Well,' she gave a little laugh, 'not as much as he should be. He's in Dublin. A lot. I mean, at the moment.'

Frank just kept smiling. Listening. Saying nothing.

'He's getting a television. For the bar.' Peggy pointed up towards the corner of the room where she intended getting one of the local lads to build a shelf for the non- existent television. She knew there'd be no point asking Jerome to do it. They'd be another year waiting for that.

Frank's eyes didn't move from her face, even to appraise her choice of situation for the proposed new television. 'And the fourth?'

Peggy squinted at him. 'Fourth?'

'You said that there were four of you.'

'Oh, yes,' she breathed. She realized instantly how unusual it was to have someone actually listen to her. Really listen to her. 'Hugo,' she said, shrugging her shoulders, 'the eldest. He's … he's in London. He doesn't have much to do with us at all, really. He left after Daddy died. Wanted out of Crumm. Understandable, I suppose.' She smiled at Frank. 'It's not exactly up for any village of the year awards.'

Frank just smiled and took a swig from his pint.

'He's the one I'm most like,' Peggy said suddenly. 'Hugo. We have the same … ' she lifted a strand of hair and looked at it before flicking it back over her shoulder. 'We look more alike. Not like … ' she gestured with the tilt of her head towards the door Carla had disappeared through. 'Herself and Jerome are more … well, they got the long legs. My mother used to say, if you stood still for a minute, that you could see Carla growing in front of your eyes. She was always a bit of a … a beanpole.'

Peggy realized then that she had been gabbing, and that Frank hadn't said a word. Even Coleman was looking at her as if she was giving him a pain in his head. She clamped her mouth closed and continued drying glasses.

'Is your mother still living?' Frank said after a moment.

'They're both dead.'

'Lord have mercy on them,' Coleman muttered into his glass.

At that moment, the door opened and five young men came into the bar, their presence washing the place with life. They each acknowledged Peggy in turn. Frank noticed the colour of her cheeks deepen as she greeted each man by name, standing a little straighter behind the bar, ready for action. The volume had been raised in the room with the arrival of the group, who seemed to be familiar to most of the regulars drinking there. The last of the men approached the bar, leaving his friends to pull some stools together around one of the tables.

'Ms. Casey,' the man greeted Peggy, who had already lifted five pint glasses onto the counter from the shelf below. His cheeks matched Peggy's for colour. The countenance of a man who spent his day outdoors.

'Fergal,' she replied. 'Five pints?'

'That's the one.' He beamed at Peggy, before noticing Frank looking at him.

'Hello,' he said. Frank nodded at him.

Fergal turned his head. 'Coleman,' he said.

Coleman grunted without looking up from his pint.

'I'll drop these down to you, Fergal,' Peggy smiled.

'Thank you, Peggy. Lads.' He saluted Frank who watched him stalk over to where his friends had congregated. The little bar almost felt full with the addition of their long limbs and loud lilting voices. Then the door opened again, and a man Frank recognized walked in. He too stopped to chat to some of the other customers before approaching the bar, his cap in his hand.

'I'll just be a second, Enda,' Peggy said to him as she set the five pints of stout on a tray. 'The usual?'

'Aye, good girl,' the man said. He stood looking about him for a moment before noticing Frank.

'Ah, Detective Sergeant,' he said, reaching into the inside pocket of his jacket. 'You had a message, sir. A ... ' he held the piece of paper at arm's length and squinted at it. 'A Garda Molloy from Dublin Castle. Phoned to inform you that Doctor ... ' he brought the paper closer to his eyes before holding it out away from him again, 'Dr. McKenna will be at the station in Crumm at ten o'clock tomorrow morning.' He looked up at Frank with a slightly concerned expression on his face. 'Does that make sense to you, sir? A Dr. McKenna?'

Frank nodded. The state pathologist. 'That's grand. Thank you, Enda.'

Ten o'clock. At least that meant he had some hope of being back up to Dublin tomorrow evening. He might be early enough to take Rose out. Make up for today. He should phone her now. He glanced up at the clock and noticed Enda O'Shea still standing there, looking at him.

'So I should have your breakfast ready what, at half-past eight, sir? Full Irish?'

Frank almost laughed until he realized that the man was serious. 'That would be fine, Enda, thank you.'

Peggy came back around the bar with an empty tray. 'Here you are, Enda,' she said, topping up a settled glass.

'God bless you, Peggy,' Enda leaned across Frank to leave some coins on the counter. 'I'll see you in the morning so, sir,' he said. 'Herself has an early appointment, so 'twill be myself looking after you.' He turned to walk away with his pint, before stopping and looking back at Frank. 'I wonder, will the Doctor require breakfast, or will we see him at all?'

'No, Enda.' Frank noticed the defeated, tired look in the man's eyes. 'Just myself.'

'Right, so,' he said turning away again and wandering off through the tables and stools like someone looking for a place to belong, hoping someone would include him somewhere. Frank saw some benevolent man half-heartedly push a stool towards Enda who bowed his head in greeting before sitting down.

'There's only one person wearing the trousers in that household, and it's not poor Enda,' Peggy said to Frank in a low voice. 'Have you met Mrs. O'Shea? Bernie?'

'I did have the pleasure,' Frank smiled at her. 'She went to great pains to inform me when I arrived that I was being given the best room in the house. Apparently, a Monsignor stayed there in 1968. Imagine.'

'Hah,' Peggy snorted. 'You'd think it was the Ritz the way she goes on. Anyway, at least you're spared her conversation over your sausages and eggs in the morning.'

They both laughed, but Frank felt a little uncomfortable and looked away first. He should really ring Rose. He pointed to the phone on the wall. 'Can I use it?' he asked.

'Of course,' Peggy lifted his empty glass and he stood down from his stool. 'Do you have change? You'll need five pence coins.'

'I do.' Frank dug his hand into his pocket. 'I suppose I'll get another pint. And,' he looked at Coleman who suddenly seemed to be interested in their conversation, 'you'll have another?' Frank asked.

'Oh, well, if the Garda Síochána is buying, I suppose I'm drinking,' came the reply.

Frank nodded at Peggy who rolled her eyes and shook her head, but said nothing.

The phone rang for almost a minute before she answered.

'Rose? I'd almost given up.'

'It's after nine, they're all in bed,' her tone was unapologetic. 'I was upstairs myself.'

'Sorry.' Frank glanced over at Peggy who seemed busy behind the bar. He turned his back to her a little. 'I haven't had a chance to call until now.' He hoped Peggy couldn't hear his lies.

45

'Where are you?' Rose was accusing. 'Are you in a pub? You sound like you're in a pub.'

'I'm just using the phone. Listen, I might be back up tomorrow. I thought, maybe, if I got back by six, well, we could do something.'

'I've plans tomorrow night.' The reply was firm. 'I'm meeting Sheila and the girls.'

'Right.'

'Right.'

'Look, Rose, I'm sorry … '

'I have to go now, Frank. Careful on the roads. I'm sure I'll see you. Whenever.'

'Look, Rose … ' He heard the receiver being hung up and the silence on the line. He waited a moment to see if she would pick up again. But nothing. She was so bloody stubborn. He sensed Peggy standing closer to him at the till.

'Ok, so. I'll see you Sunday,' he said loudly into the handset. 'Bye so.' He hung the receiver gently back on the cradle. Shit. He was going to have to do something about Rose. He knew she was disappointed about the weekend, but he needed to work. And he needed someone who could understand that. Support. He needed a little support. He turned to walk back around to his stool, when he noticed another man, arm stretched out before him, leaning heavily on the bar next to Coleman. His head was bowed low, like a priest listening to Coleman's confession. Coleman appeared to be talking slowly, importantly, basking in the audience. Peggy set his pint down on a coaster and shrugged her shoulders in apology.

'Ah now, Doctor. This is the man himself,' Coleman said as Frank sat back down on his stool. 'Detective Sergeant, this is Doctor. Doctor, Detective Sergeant.'

Frank regarded the man who was of Coleman's own vintage, although darker in complexion and with a full head of greasy, liquorice-like hair. He noticed that their clothes might have been got from the same bin bag, although the second man's shoes were of black leather, polished to a sheen that Frank's superior officers would have been proud of. The man stuck out a grubby, wizened hand to Frank, who shook it tentatively.

'The Detective Sergeant is looking for assistance with the discovery down at the lake,' Coleman said slowly. 'You might find that Doctor here is a good source of local information, Detective Sergeant, he being of a family that goes back four generations in the area.'

Doctor smiled dreamily, his eyes closed, his arm leaning on the bar all the while. Frank thought that one local nutter's opinion was quite enough in any investigation, but he could see what was going on.

'You'll have a pint, sir?' he sighed.

'Oh, well if you are offering, that would be most agreeable, thank you sir.' Doctor's eyes stayed shut, even as he spoke.

Frank gestured at Peggy and looked back at his new drinking companion. He noticed the man's grimy fingernails. 'So you were the village GP?' he asked, his disbelief audible.

'Not at all,' Peggy almost laughed, earning herself a sudden glare from the dark-haired man. 'Doctor is his name. Or at least, that's what he is called. He's certainly not a doctor. And,' she looked at the man, who was swaying slightly where he stood between Coleman and Frank, 'he should not be taking pints from visitors to the place. Unless he really is in a position to help the Sergeant. Are you, Doc? Have you something to add to the investigation? Can you assist Frank with his enquiries?'

Frank gazed at Peggy as she scolded the old man next to him. He liked that she was willing to jump to his assistance. Not that he needed her to. He could handle two old drunks by himself, no problem. But she was so … feisty. He liked that. And she'd called him Frank. He liked that too.

'Now, young wan.' Coleman evidently could see a threat to his evening of free drink, and he was unwilling to let it go easily. 'Doctor is so named as he is the seventh son of a seventh son. A gifted individual. A special soul. The seventh son of a seventh son is exactly the person you want to help you in your investigation. In any investigation.'

'Pah.' Peggy wrenched the tap down; filling the man's pint glass with none of the care Frank had seen her take with every other drink that evening. 'Well, use your powers now, Doctor, and tell the Detective what you can. If that's anything at all. Because this is the last pint he'll be buying you in this establishment.'

Frank saw her glance at him quickly, her cheeks flushed. He acknowledged her intervention with a quick wink, which seemed to make her blush even more.

'Doctor worked on the graveyard also, Detective Sergeant.' Coleman rested an elbow on the counter and looked across his friend at Frank. 'He drove the hearse back and forth to the new cemetery. Is that not the way it was, Doctor?'

'It was, it was,' the man replied. Frank noted his canny ability to reach for his pint, even with his eyes closed.

'Each remains was afforded a new coffin, and that coffin was lifted into the hearse to be brought up the hill.'

Frank listened to Coleman talk, but he knew now that the body at the lake could not be from the old graveyard. It was in the wrong location, on the wrong side of the valley. And the sacking. Something about the sacking was bothering him, but he couldn't think what. It was as if he recognized the material from somewhere, but his mind wouldn't let him remember.

'What's the lake called?' he asked.

'What do you mean?' Peggy seemed to work continuously behind the bar as she spoke. She reminded Frank of a dancer, graceful and assured, as she never ceased wiping surfaces, rinsing glasses and tidying them away.

'Well, there's no name given to it on the map. It just says Crumm Reservoir.'

'Yeah,' Peggy said. 'That's its official name, I think.'

'There was no name given to it,' Coleman growled. 'Those Dublin boys thought they would graciously allow the local people

48

to name it, but as you might imagine, no one that was left behind had much of a stomach for the job. So it was never officially named.'

'The anglers call it Glanaphuca Lake,' Peggy said. 'That's what you see on their posters and whatnot. But I think they just made that up. It sounds more inviting than Crumm Reservoir when they're advertising their competitions, I suppose.'

'Glanaphuca,' Frank said.

'I know,' Peggy smiled. 'Valley of the ghosts. Not the most beguiling name they could have come up with.'

But certainly appropriate in light of current events, Frank thought. 'Is there any chance you might recall whether any person went missing in the locality over the years, Coleman?' Frank leaned across Doctor, ignoring him. He was fairly sure that even if the man had any information, his current condition meant it would be unreliable, at best.

Coleman furrowed his brow and stared off over the bar. 'No, no. Can you recall, Doctor?' He turned to his friend briefly, and then proceeded to ignore him himself. 'No, no. No missing persons that I recall. Do you mean in the last few years, sir?'

Frank paused. He had his own ideas about the vintage of the find, but until the pathologist saw it, he didn't like to make assumptions. 'Possibly. Possibly from before the flooding of the valley.'

Coleman rubbed his whiskers on his chin. 'Well, a lot of people moved on. Moved out. It's possible someone was thought to have left around that time, where in actual fact they were buried on the shoreline.' He pushed another cigarette out of the box and put it unlit into his mouth. 'So you suspect some treachery, Detective Sergeant?'

Frank leaned back on his stool. 'Not necessarily,' he said. 'Until the Doctor … the State Pathologist … ' he added quickly, 'until Dr. McKenna sees the body, it will be impossible to say how she died.'

'Ah.' Coleman seemed to give up on waiting for someone to strike a match for him, and he picked up the matchbox himself and shook it. 'So it is the body of a woman, sir?'

Frank drained his pint. 'We can't say for certain yet,' he said quietly. He glanced around the room, but could see no sign of Peggy. It was time for him to leave. He didn't think Coleman could enlighten him any further. Not at this stage in the evening. He'd wait to see what the pathologist had to say in the morning. If necessary, he could look at interviewing people after that. He stood down from his stool. He knew he was stalling to see Peggy again, to say thank you, or goodbye, or something. There was still no sign of her. He noticed a line of rusty metal objects nailed to a beam in the ceiling, just above where he had been sitting. They looked like tools. Farm tools and blades. Two large serving ladles hung further along.

'Treasures from the lake.'

Frank started as Peggy suddenly appeared beside him, carrying a tray of glasses of various sizes, all with a white foamy residue inside. She set it down on the counter and looked up at the line of metal objects.

'Every so often, something washes up on the shoreline. A kitchen utensil from one of the houses. Part of some farm machinery. There's even part of a loom there.' She pointed up at a flat metal bar, punctured at both ends with small holes. 'The fishermen bring them in sometimes. We hang them there. Out of … ' she pushed her hair back from her face, 'out of respect, I suppose.'

Frank noticed she was blushing again, as she walked around the counter and began to rinse the glasses.

'They're like little reminders of what happened here.' She stopped for a moment. 'Like little whispers from the past. You never know what the lake is going to reveal.'

They stood looking at each other for a moment. Then suddenly, the door behind Peggy opened and Carla walked through from the house. Frank noticed her face was scrubbed clean and her hair was tied back from her face in a severe ponytail.

'Detective. You're still here.' She took a beer bottle from the shelf and opened it in one fluid movement.

50

'I'm just leaving, actually.' Frank looked at Peggy. 'Thank you for your hospitality. It's likely I'll be back in the morning with Garda O'Dowd. We might have a few questions for you. Or your brother, if he's around.'

'You'll be lucky,' Carla said from behind her sister, and she swigged from the neck of the bottle. Frank tried to ignore her.

'Nothing serious. We'll be asking the same questions of all the business people in the area. Nothing to worry about.'

'Of course, Detective, of course. I'll be here all day. Jerome should be in around lunchtime. We will be serving lunch. From noon. Just … just if it suited you, of course.'

Frank smiled at her. 'Thank you, Peggy.'

Carla snorted into her bottle.

'Ms. Casey,' Frank said to her, and turned to leave. 'Gentlemen,' he said in the direction of the two men at the bar, and walked halfway across the room before stopping. He turned back around and addressed Coleman, who didn't lift his head from his pint. 'You'll be around tomorrow, Coleman?'

'I will,' Coleman said into his glass. 'Sure amn't I always around?'

'You might walk with me to the lake in the morning? You may perhaps be able to cast some light on the situation? Or at least give me your own take on the matter. You having all the local knowledge, and such.'

Coleman turned stiffly on his seat. 'I will, of course, assist An Garda Síochána in whatever way the Detective feels I might be in a position to.'

Frank nodded. Something was still bugging him, and he couldn't think what it was. And that was bothering him even more. Something someone had said earlier. He lifted his hand in recognition of Enda O'Shea who, seeing him leave, had raised his pint to him, and he walked past the yellowing photographs of grinning men holding dead fish, and out of The Angler's Rest.

He was glad to get out into the cool night air. He needed to think. He sat in his car for a moment, looking up at the front of the pub, with its whitewashed walls and glass lanterns hanging either side of the wooden front door. He thought of the two women inside. Crumm was not the place for a woman like Peggy. She was so much more than Crumm. He could see what a great job she was doing with the family business, but even so, it must be a lonely existence for her. And she seemed to him like the kind of girl who was meant for bigger things. Better things. But then, who was he to say? Maybe running her family business was what Peggy wanted from life. He knew plenty of girls who had never left his own village in Galway. Maybe everything Peggy wanted was here in Crumm.

Frank turned the key in the ignition and put the Capri into reverse. His thoughts turned to the body at the lake. He'd go down there now. Check on Garda O'Dowd and the young O'Malley lad. Maybe he should have moved the body today, but something had told him to wait. There could be clues to the mystery in the mud on the shoreline, and he was loath to disturb it. Better to let the doctor examine the lot before removing her. The Doctor. Frank shook his head, thinking of the other dirty, unkempt man holding up the bar in Casey's. There really is one in every village, he thought, as he drove off through the darkness in the direction of the lake.

EIGHT

'Goodnight, lads. Goodnight.' Peggy pushed the old door closed behind the last few customers to leave. There were always the same few left till the end, nursing the dregs of their pints, the same few who apparently would rather sit in an empty bar well past midnight than meet with whatever waited for them at home. Belligerent wives in some cases, Peggy knew. But in others, there was only the quiet of the four walls waiting, and for those, mostly older men, Peggy understood the dread her calling time brought on. Still, it had to be done. She could hear them standing, talking, outside the door as she heaved her shoulder against it, pushing a worn brass bolt across at the same time. She stood back and kicked at another bolt closer to the floor. Walking back through the bar, she collected the last few empty glasses and brought them to the counter. Maura could do them in the morning. She still had the whole kitchen to clean, and she was tired. She rattled a window lock, and took one last look around the place before flicking the light switch on the wall.

She hoped Carla had gone to bed. She didn't know what to say to her. As it happened, it was Carla's back she saw on entering the old kitchen, as she stood near the sink rubbing something with a tea towel. She seemed not to hear Peggy as she came in.

Peggy looked round the room. All evidence of the stew and the accompanying mess had miraculously disappeared.

'You cleaned up!' She realized a second too late that her tone would not be well received.

'It's not like I've never cleaned this kitchen before,' Carla spun around, jolted from her reverie, her eyes glaring. She might have noticed the exhaustion in her sister's eyes, or been startled by the pallor of her usually ruddy cheeks, but Carla seemed to pause, before setting the plate she was drying down on the worktop with a sigh. 'Want a mug of tea?'

Peggy sensed the olive branch being offered and she took it.

'Yes. I would love a mug of tea.' She pulled a heavy wooden chair from beneath the large kitchen table that dominated the room, and sat down. It was only when she took the weight off her feet that she realized how exhausted she was.

Carla busied herself at the range. 'I was going to have a sandwich. I haven't eaten all evening. Do you want one?'

Even if Peggy hadn't been hungry, she wouldn't have turned her sister down. Carla rarely went out of her way for anyone, least of all Peggy. And a sandwich meant her time and company, possibly even her conversation. 'That would be great,' she said and watched as her sister put ham and tomato on slices of white, buttered bread. Carla put the teapot and the food on the table and sat down opposite Peggy. They ate in silence for a moment, the ticking of the clock and the odd creaking from the old Aga the only other noises in the room.

'So Jerome will be back in the morning?' Carla said, at last.

'Lunchtime,' Peggy said, her mouth full.

'Hmm.' Carla was disapproving. 'He shouldn't leave you here on your own so much.'

'You were here.'

'Yeah, today. But how long is he gone?'

Peggy didn't want to get into this. 'Wednesday,' she said, hoping the confession would get lost in her mug of tea.

54

'Since Wednesday?' Carla's eyes were wide. Peggy noticed that the heavy eyeliner she was never seen without in public seemed to have been washed away.

Carla looked as if she wanted to say more, but had thought the better of it. She swallowed a mouthful of tea instead. 'He shouldn't leave you like that,' she muttered.

Peggy waited, unsure what to say. She worried about Jerome too. She wanted to talk to someone about him. But Carla could be so critical. And she could do without her brother and sister spending the weekend at each other's throats.

'He can't go on like this,' Carla seemed to be talking to herself now. 'I don't care what he … ' she stopped suddenly, and looked up at Peggy across the table.

'He's getting the television,' Peggy blurted.

Carla looked unimpressed at this piece of information, but then she leaned back in her chair and sighed. 'Yeah?'

'Yeah.' Peggy was acutely aware that her enthusiasm was not shared by her sister, but there was little unusual in that. 'I think it'll help. You know, there are plenty in the village with no television themselves. They'll all come in to watch the big things. It'll pay for itself, I know it will.'

Carla stared over at her sister, scorn contorting her face. 'What big things?'

'You know,' Peggy played with the handle of her mug. 'When there's a big news story. Like Dev's funeral. They were all crowded into Bridie Hennessy's for that. Or … or the big matches.' She looked up at Carla, vindicated. 'If we had a television this Sunday, we could show the All-Ireland. Can you imagine the crowd in for that?' Peggy's eyes glazed over as she pictured Casey's crammed with punters in to see the match, some standing outside looking in the windows for lack of space. She'd have to hire one of the local lads to help her behind the bar; the place would be so busy. They could have sandwiches made; ready to sell at half-time, or perhaps after the match concluded. She pictured it all, and glowed with satisfaction as she sat in the quiet kitchen. Then she realized that Detective Sergeant Frank Ryan was in her daydream too, sitting at the bar, shouting at the imaginary television, cheering the Dubs on. She shook herself from her fantasy. What was she doing? Frank wouldn't be there. Even if by some miracle Jerome did bring the television back with him tomorrow, Frank wouldn't be here on Sunday. She glanced up at Carla, almost expecting her to have read her mind and be ready with another taunt, but Carla seemed to be lost in her own thoughts. Peggy summoned all the courage within, and attempted to transform it into words in her mouth. There was so much she wanted to talk to Carla about. What exactly was going on? Why was Tom Devereaux calling her on Friday night, drunk? Tom Devereaux, her boss? Tom Devereaux, a married man? She willed Carla to look up, to see the questions in her eyes so that she wouldn't have to articulate them. But Carla's gaze didn't move from the mug in front of her.

'So,' Peggy said.

Carla looked at her hard. 'So?'

Peggy opened her mouth but closed it again. 'The body thing's weird, isn't it?' she said, at last.

Carla looked back down at her mug, and Peggy exhaled heavily.

'Yeah. I suppose it is.' Carla picked at a piece of nail varnish that was flaking off her thumbnail. 'I wonder who it is. Was.'

'Could be an IRA thing,' Peggy said. She was glad to have some neutral topic of conversation to discuss with her sister, even if it was a dead body. 'Maybe it's a Loyalist. Or a snitch. They've killed people like that before, and buried their bodies.'

'Ah Peggy. Don't be daft.'

Peggy shrugged her shoulders. It was well known that the hills around Ballyknock and Crumm had been notorious during the civil war, littered with safe- houses, and scenes of infamous skirmishes between the Staters and the Republicans.

'Maybe it's older?' she said. 'From the twenties?'

'Huh.' Carla stood suddenly, the scraping of her chair legs on the tiled floor shattering the calm of the room. 'It's probably just some fool that refused to move when they flooded the valley.' She brought her plate over to the sink. 'Some stubborn eejit that sat in her house as the water rose around her ankles until she had no choice but to go under with the rest of it.' She stood at the door leading to the rest of the house and pulled her cardigan tightly around herself. 'Or some idiot, like Coleman Quirke, who thought that a moonlit walk over the bridge after ten pints was a great idea.'

The gentle banter was evidently over. Peggy just sipped her tea and let her sister rant and bluster.

'There'll be no great story. It'll be no one famous or important. And your Detective Sergeant will go back to Dublin, and you'll never hear from him again, Peg. So don't get your hopes up. Right?'

Peggy tried her utmost to keep all expression from her face. 'Right,' she said.

Carla paused a moment, and for a second, Peggy thought she was considering sitting down again. But then her sister yanked the door handle and turned on her heel. 'Goodnight, so,' she said as she disappeared into the house.

Peggy sat unmoving for a moment. She had read in one of her magazines that it was good practice to breathe slowly and count silently to ten when you wanted to stop yourself from screaming and punching someone. She almost had to marvel at how Carla could, without a word having been spoken on the matter, find the fontanel of her thoughts, and stamp up and down on it unabashedly.

Frank. Of course, she had thought him attractive. Any normal girl would. She was fairly convinced that Carla herself had had an appreciation of his presence in The Angler's Rest that evening. But had she really thought more of it? Maybe Carla had been one step ahead of her subconscious. She seemed to have worked through their attraction, affair, and Peggy's broken heart before Peggy herself had had the chance to mull over the possibility of it.

Well, maybe Carla was right. This was Crumm, after all. Not the type of place where handsome men from Dublin came to find love. It was Crumm, where nothing ever happened; a village forever anchored to a painful and brutal past, the truth of which seemed to cast a lake-shaped shadow on the people who lived there.

Peggy sat in the quiet kitchen and thought about Coleman. It was rare to get more than a few sentences out of him on any occasion, and she had never heard him tell the story of the evacuation before. She had, of course, been aware of the history of the place; how their pub had once stood more than half a mile from the river water that now lapped less than one hundred feet away. But that is what it had always been. History. Before her time. She had only been a baby when the valley was flooded, and she could remember it no other way. Her own family had not been adversely affected by the dam; indeed, the new lake had brought opportunity and business to her father. But although she had known that some of the older people living in Crumm had once lived in the valley the lake now filled, she had never really stopped to consider what it might have been like for them to pack up their belongings and walk away from their houses and farms, knowing they were soon to be destroyed.

The washed-outs, they had been dubbed: Coleman and his older brother, old Mrs. King, Mr. Murphy out the Ballyknock road; there were very few left, really. But then, who would want to live next to a lake, knowing that your home was at the bottom of it?

Peggy drained her tea. It was ironic, how so many had been forced from the place not a quarter century before, and yet she had somehow managed to get tethered here herself. And while some days Peggy loved being the proprietress of The Angler's Rest, on others she worried that's all she would ever be.

She thought about Hugo, and how apparently easily he had set down the reins of the place and walked away into a new life. There was no stopping her doing the same.

She thought about Frank. Sometimes it took an outsider to illuminate the familiar, to show it up for what it was. He reminded her of a boy she had studied with in catering college. They shared the same fair hair. There had been a time when she had entertained the idea of going away with him, to London maybe, or even America. They might have found their own place. Their own story. She hadn't thought of that boy in months. He'd gone to Boston not long after her father had died, and she had moved back to Crumm to manage the bar. He had sent her a postcard from a very fancy looking establishment called Parker House, where he was working as an assistant manager in housekeeping. It had sounded very grand to her. It had sounded a long way from Crumm.

She stood and brought her empty plate and mug over to the sink. She could smell smoke wafting from her clothes and her hair as she moved. She needed a bath, but she was too tired. And the smoke never went away anyway. Her lasting memory of her father was his warm, comforting smell of beer, and tobacco, and turf fires. That smell never shifted. It became part of you. It had become part of him. And as long as she ran The Angler's Rest in Crumm, Peggy knew that she would be no different.

NINE

Saturday, 27th September 1975
Frank could feel Bernie O'Shea's homemade black pudding
swilling around in his stomach. Crouched below him, the State
Pathologist, Dr. Aloysius McKenna was using what looked like a
metal spatula to push back the wet sand from the area of the body
already exposed. He muttered to himself as he worked; nothing
Frank could decipher. Every now and then he would stop, lean
back, and gesture at Garda O'Dowd, who would move in a little
closer and take a photograph with a Nikon 35mm. He said nothing
to Frank as he worked; indeed, he had hardly uttered two words
to Frank since they had met for the first time at the station that
morning. As one of the youngest Detective Sergeants in the force,
Frank knew he looked just a little too young to be taken seriously
on the job. Respect came with age in this game. In that, he and
Michael O'Dowd had common ground, he thought, looking at
the guard as he held the doctor's camera as if it was made of
eggshell. Dr. McKenna stood up and scribbled in a hardback
notepad, which he leaned on his upper thigh. He continued to
mutter all the while.

Frank used the opportunity to take in the changing scenery
around him. When they had arrived that morning, the early sun

had cast shadows on the lake and the shore where they stood, but now, under the clear sky of late morning, there was nowhere to hide. The still air sat heavy on the lake water, the tall evergreens towering silently above their heads. It felt to him as if the whole place was holding its breath, waiting to see what awful truth might be disinterred from its bleak beauty. Downstream, he could make out what looked like a line of boulders, disappearing into the still water. The arrangement made no sense to him. He made a mental note to examine it more closely later.

Across the other side of the lake, he could make out a dilapidated estate house, partially hidden by trees. The old manor. Its windows resembled eyes, peeking out across at him through the branches, half afraid of what it might see. There was certainly no way the body that lay here, ten feet from where he now stood, could have been from the old graveyard near the estate.

'It's P and T.' Dr. McKenna suddenly addressed Frank. He was kneeling on a piece of cardboard he must have brought with him. He pointed at the body in the sand. 'Jute. It appears the deceased was buried here in a post bag.' He used what looked to him like a wire brush to remove some of the wet sand further down the length of the body. 'You might be able to make out the lettering here?' He glanced up at him. 'The deceased, female it would seem at this stage, appears to have been put, post-mortem, into a Post and Telegraphs sack, and buried here.'

Just then, two figures standing on elevated ground on the shoreline caught Frank's eye. One was the driver of the hearse that was parked nearby, ready to remove the remains to the church, where the local priest had offered Frank the use of a room should he need it. The other was Coleman.

'We should be able to get an approximate date fairly quickly from the style of the bag.' Dr. McKenna seemed to be talking to the body now, addressing it like a doctor might a patient, gently explaining a procedure; what would happen next. Frank kept his eyes fixed on Coleman.

Then the doctor stood, and both Frank and Garda O'Dowd turned to him.

'I've seen all I need to here. Let's get her up to the sacristy, and I can get a better look at her. If needs be, we'll get the lot up to Dublin tonight, or in the morning.'

'Right.' Frank noticed that Garda O'Dowd was looking at him in his needy way, waiting for direction.

'Let the undertaker know the doctor is finished, Michael,' he said. 'They're to bring her to the church. Father Francis is expecting her there.'

The doctor proceeded to put the tools he had been using back into a large leather bag. 'They're to take the remains as they are, in the sack,' he said. 'Make sure there is no interference with it. It's to all go into the box. Keep that,' he gestured to the camera Garda O'Dowd was still holding. 'You'll take two final pictures of the site when the remains are removed. 'Now, Detective Sergeant. Perhaps we might find someone to make us a cup of tea in this Godforsaken place?'

Frank bristled at his tone, and then wondered immediately why he cared. He glanced at Michael who just nodded quickly at him. Then he took one last look at the body in the sand. Whatever peace the creature had had since being left here was being well and truly disturbed now. A third of the sand covering the shape was now pushed back, the sacking clear for all to see. A postbag containing the crumpled body of some poor person, some poor girl. Suddenly, a warm wind blew across the lake, apparently from nowhere, and he looked up to see the trees near the manor swaying, revealing the house more fully. Then he turned quickly and looked back up the shoreline.

But Coleman was gone.

TEN

By the time Carla appeared in the kitchen, groggy and dishevelled, Peggy had already been up and working for three hours. Two large pans of cottage pie were set out on the table and Peggy was standing at the sink, stripping cooking apples of their skins.

She looked up at her sister. 'Morning.'

'Meh.' Carla lifted a kettle from where it sat on the range, letting it drop with a clatter. Overnight, she seemed to have morphed back into the teenager who used to haunt the kitchen late on Saturday mornings, in the very same dressing gown, now worn and bally, and inappropriate-looking somehow. Peggy had always been scared of that Carla in her youth, and she was no less wary now. Before the silence went on long enough to mean anything, Maura appeared at the door to the bar and saved her.

'You've a few in here now, Peggy. Oh good morning, Carla.' Maura opened the door more fully and came through into the kitchen. 'Do you get up for a while every day to grace us with your presence?'

Peggy heard the softness cosseting Maura's sarcasm, and she watched her pat Carla's shoulder before going over to the kettle and giving it a rattle. Apparently forgetting all about the customers in the bar, Maura proceeded to spoon tea leaves from a brightly coloured tin into a mug.

'And how are those Wexford brats treating you this weather?'

'Badly,' Carla said to her with a smile.

She wouldn't smile at me, Peggy thought as she wiped her hands on her apron. 'I'll see to them inside, so,' she said.

'Good girl.' Maura sat herself down at the table across from Carla.

Peggy sighed and left them to it. In the bar, two men were sitting at one of the tables, a large tackle box on the floor next to them.

'Good morning, gentlemen,' Peggy said. 'What can I get you?'

'Aye, lass. We're just going to take the edge off before we go out. Two pints should do it. And maybe two small ones while you're at it.'

Peggy nodded. The men had the look of a couple of naughty children left for the day without supervision. Which is what they were, she supposed. They're all the same, she thought to herself, just as the front door opened and Frank walked in, accompanied by an older, grey-haired man, smartly dressed in a shirt and sleeveless jumper. The man looked vaguely familiar to Peggy, and then she remembered seeing his photograph in the newspaper. Frank smiled as he approached the bar. Peggy cursed her stomach for flipping as it did.

'Good morning, Peggy,' he said.

'Detective Sergeant. You're in early.'

'Yes, well,' he eyed the two half-pulled pints in Peggy's hands. 'Not for one of those, unfortunately. We've been down at the lake.' He gestured over to where the other gentleman was settling himself at a small table. 'I was wondering if it might be possible to get tea or coffee for Dr. McKenna. He drove up very early from Cork, and I don't think he's had breakfast. We're just waiting on the hearse to move the body up to the church.'

'Of course,' Peggy smiled, 'just give me a second and I'll be out with a tray.'

She set the two pints down in front of the fishermen, stealing a glance at Dr. McKenna as she did, and went through to the kitchen. Five minutes later she returned with a pot of tea, a pot of coffee, two china mugs, and a plate of buttered brown bread.

'Will this do the Doctor?' she asked, setting the tray on the table in front of them.

'That's great, Peggy.' Frank smiled. 'Thank you.'

The doctor ignored her. He lifted the lids on the pots, sniffing through a turned-up nose at the steam released. Peggy nodded at Frank and left them alone. As she walked away, she thought she heard someone, somewhere, singing loudly. Just then, there was a banging on the front door, and after a few failed attempts, it opened heavily, to reveal a fresh-faced Jerome, carrying a large, cardboard box that made him stumble and sway. He was singing as he came in, and when his eyes fell on Peggy, he increased the volume.

'*Oh I'll have bad times, and you'll have good times. Doin' things that I don't understand.*' He grinned at her over the top of the box. When he got as far as the first bar room table, he set it down, slowly, carefully. '*But if you love me, you'll forgive me.*' He spread his arms wide, and beamed at Peggy as if he might be expecting a round of applause.

'Well?' He tipped his head towards his prize. 'Who's your favourite brother now? Come on, don't be shy. You can tell me. Am I amazing? Or what?' He gestured to the box with both hands. 'You're thinking; he's fantastic? The best brother a girl could have? Come on, Peg. Put it here. Gimme some lovin'.' He held out his arms wide for her.

Standing there in the bar, clad in his blue bell-bottoms and floral shirt, it was difficult not to smile, but Peggy tried hard not to. Instead she went to investigate the box. She was afraid to hope.

'Is it?'

'It is.'

She moved her hand over the cardboard as though it might have been mink.

'And is it really … '

'Colour. Yes. Nothing but the best for Casey's Bar. And for my beloved sister. Of course.'

Peggy clapped her hands together. 'Oh Jer!' She spun around and almost toppled him with the hug. 'I forgive you for abandoning me every other week, and for leaving me to deal with all the shite here. You're not really the neglectful arse everyone says you are.'

'Like who?' Jerome pulled back from her slightly. 'Who says that?'

'Oh, I don't know. Carla.'

'Ah, there's a surprise.'

'And Maura.'

'Maura would never say such a thing.' He disengaged himself from Peggy, and straightened the enormous collar of his shirt, beaming to himself. 'Maura loves me like her own.'

'Yeah,' Peggy said, but she was no longer really listening. She was looking from the cardboard box to the space in the corner up near the ceiling where she had envisaged the television going. 'Do ya think it'll fit okay?'

'Ah, yeah. I'll sort it out later. Right now, my stomach's back in Ballyknock. I'm going inside to get a sandwich.'

He lifted the box once more and brought it over to a small table in the corner of the bar. Peggy followed him, guiding the precious goods all the way. She couldn't believe it was finally here. A television. A colour television.

Jerome jerked his head. 'Who are the two women drinking tea in the corner?'

Peggy swung around to see if someone had joined Frank's table, but it was just Frank and the doctor there still. She waited until Jerome had settled the box safely, before whacking him hard over the shoulder.

'Have a bit of respect, boy,' she whispered. 'That is Detective Sergeant Frank Ryan from Dublin, and the man with him is only the State Pathologist, Dr. Aloysius McKenna. You may not be aware, but while you were up in Dublin enjoying yourself, some drama has been unfolding here.'

'What drama?' Jerome looked indignant, but he lowered his voice.

'A body,' Peggy whispered.

'A what?'

'Shh!' Peggy glanced over her shoulder at Frank's table, but the two men appeared to be taking no heed of them. 'A body was found at the lake. Thursday. Some fishermen noticed it, and the Garda were called up from Dublin. And then the State Pathologist.'

'Jesus.'

'I know. Everyone just assumed it was very old. Well it was covered by the lake water until this summer. Anyway,' she rubbed the top of the television box again with her finger, 'they're removing it to the church this morning. I suppose they'll know more after that.' She looked at Jerome, eyes wide, and lowered her voice even further. 'I bet it's an IRA informer. It could be, couldn't it? Or something like that?'

'Wow.' Jerome looked genuinely shocked. 'I don't know, Peg. Maybe. Jaysus.' He ran his fingers through his long, floppy hair. 'Bodies aren't the kind of thing you expect to be hearing about. Not around here.'

Just then Frank rose from his table and approached the two of them. He nodded at Jerome.

'Thanks for that, Peggy. I'll settle with you now, if that's okay.'

'Oh, not at all Frank. It was just tea. Please, take it with our compliments. As a thank you for, well for all you are doing. Frank,' she turned to her brother but avoided his eyes; 'this is my brother, Jerome.'

'Frank Ryan,' Frank extended his hand.

'Detective Sergeant Frank Ryan,' Peggy corrected.

'Detective Sergeant.'

Peggy couldn't be sure if Jerome's tone was mocking, but she had an inkling it was.

'Jerome Casey. I hear you've been busy down at the lake. Well, at least you've the weather for it. I don't suppose yourself and your esteemed colleague will have a chance to go fishing while you're here? It's quite the spot for the pike.'

Peggy's cheeks burned at Jerome's conduct. She saw Frank observing, taking it all in; Jerome's flamboyant clothes, his platform shoes, his glossy hair. She willed him to stop flicking it back over his shoulder as he did. The contrast between the two men was stark. There was probably less than five years between them, but they could not have been more different. Frank's understated, fair, rugged appearance made Jerome's dark, girlish looks even more pronounced, his hips more slender, his shirt more garish, his eyelashes longer.

Frank looked at Peggy. 'Not this weekend,' he said. 'Thanks for the tea, Peggy. Maybe I'll see you later in the day, depending how things pan out over at the church?'

'Sure. Of course, Frank. If there's anything we can do to help … ' she glanced at her brother who was staring with open disdain at Frank.

Aloysius McKenna collected his things, and walked to the door ahead of Frank, without acknowledging either of them. The instant the door closed heavily behind them, Peggy turned on Jerome.

'What the hell was that?'

Jerome was glowering at the shut door. 'What the hell was what?'

Peggy clenched her fingers at her side. 'Why were you being rude to Frank?'

'What are you talking about?' Jerome crossed his arms in front of him. 'What's he to you? He's just a bloody Garda, same as all the other bloody Gardai. What do you care how I speak to him?'

Peggy was momentarily taken aback. Her usually relaxed, cheerful brother seemed to have been replaced by a bitter, resentful person she hardly recognized. She noticed the two fishermen stand from their seats and gather their equipment together. She tried to temper her voice.

'It's just; he's done nothing to us. He's only been doing his job down at the lake. And he's been very … pleasant.'

Not for the first time, Peggy swore to herself that, if there were ever some operation to cure blushing, she would be first in the queue for it.

Jerome ran his fingers through his hair. 'Oh Peggy, please don't go falling for a bloody Garda.' He shook his head at her. 'That's all this family needs. A bloody Garda. Holy Christ.'

He laughed a manic sort of a laugh, and turned his back on his sister.

'Don't walk away from me, Jerome. Jerome?'

Peggy nodded at the two fishermen as they passed her with their eyes on the floor, apparently eager to remove themselves from the premises. 'Thank you. Thank you, gentlemen,' she called after them. One of them glanced back at her as he tried to pull the front door behind himself. He looked a bit scared. She swung back around towards her brother as soon as the door banged shut.

'Jerome?'

'What Peggy? What? What is it?' Jerome swivelled on his platform shoes. His eyes seemed as dark as his hair. Standing there in front of the counter, Peggy saw how ridiculous his clothes were, how out of place for The Angler's Rest. He was like a tropical flower all alone in a field of winter barley. Peggy suddenly felt very sad.

'What's wrong with you, Jerome?' she said. 'Why are you so angry? What, is there something going on? Something wrong?' Peggy could almost hear the unnatural silence in the room as her heart seemed to stop beating.

'There's nothing wrong with me, Peggy. Nothing at all. I'm fine.' He spat his words out, although Peggy sensed that his anger was not directed at herself. 'The problem is not with me. It's other people.' He looked down at his shoes. 'And people like your pal Frank there,' he nodded towards the empty table where the tea things still sat. 'He's the problem, Peggy. Not me. So,' he turned towards the door leading to the kitchen, 'I suggest you find someone else to moon over. Stay away from the Gardaí.' He muttered something that sounded like 'pigs' under his breath as he walked away.

It took Peggy a moment to find her voice; such was her shock at Jerome's tone.

'Well he was a paying customer last night,' she yelled at the door as it swung closed behind her brother. 'Not that it might mean anything to you, Jerome Casey. But it does to me! I try not to insult them while their money is good!'

Her barrage echoed a little around the empty bar. She stood facing the counter, her mind's eye seeing through into the kitchen where her siblings were. The anger that coloured her cheeks and closed her fists radiated out through her eyes and into that kitchen and the people in there. Why was this so bloody hard? She expected aggravation from Carla, but now Jerome too? What was his problem? Neither of them ever looked around the bar and said, 'Nice job, Peggy'. 'Thanks for all the hard work, Peggy. Or 'Wow, Peggy, you were right about the food. Our bar could be just some hole in the middle of nowhere, but you have really put us on the map with the local tourist trade. Well done, Peggy. Daddy would have been proud.' All she ever got was criticism and abuse. She was sick of the lot of them. Why did they bother coming back at the weekends when all they did was drive her mad? She would be better off employing one of the lads from the village to help her out. She could send them each a cheque for their share of the business every month and pay herself a proper salary. That's what she should do. Carla could live in bloody Wexford and Jerome could get himself a flat in Dublin and stay there. Hugo was the only helpful one of the lot of them, and he only came home twice a year.

She directed an animated growl at the door from behind gritted teeth, and felt the better for it. She pulled out a stool and sat down with a sigh that was too big for a twenty-three-year-old's lungs. Her eyes drifted over to the large cardboard box that sat quietly on the corner table, the sole witness to her frustrations. She looked up at the reflection of the empty bar in the mirror behind the till. Then she caught sight of her own reflection looking back at her. She sighed heavily again. For all she loved them, her family were the bane of her life. And that was a fact that was apparently never going to change.

ELEVEN

Frank hated churches. He hated everything about them: the beady-eyed statues, the crucifixes, the hard wooden hassocks, the sounds, the smells. Particularly the smells. Old wood and candle wax and musty garbs. And incense. Especially the incense. One sniff of the stuff, even from the last pew of the church during a funeral, and Frank was transported back to his youth, when he had reluctantly served as an altar boy every Sunday and most mornings during Lent. That smell was as powerful as any magic potion. And that's what the lot of it was, in his opinion. Hocus pocus. He tried to respect other people and their traditions, but it meant nothing to him.

But that smell. Even here in the relatively secular surroundings of the church sacristy, his nose could pick up on a hint of frank-incense and it made him jumpy. He noticed Dr. McKenna raising an eyebrow at him, not for the first time, and he stopped pacing the room and leaned heavily against an old wooden cupboard.

'Everything all right, Detective Sergeant?'

'Yes, doctor. Of course.' Frank coughed. 'Unless I can assist you there in any way?'

But the doctor had resumed ignoring Frank, and was mumbling to himself again, just as he had down at the lake.

When they arrived at the church less than twenty minutes earlier, they were greeted at the door by a balding, middle-aged priest in a plain black garb. Before he had spoken to either of them, he had said something in Latin over the coffin being borne by two of the undertaker's men. They had followed the priest through a side door and into the room, where two tables had been arranged in the middle of the floor. The coffin had been let down on one. Under Dr. McKenna's instruction, the two young men had unscrewed the lid and lifted a sheet, holding the remains, out and onto the second table. The contents of the sheet seemed ridiculously light and small; too small to be a real person. The postbag was very obvious now it was free of the silty sand, for the most part, although some still clung wetly to it in places. The letters 'P&T' were evident, and the indignity of it made Frank's heart feel heavy. Dr. McKenna had taken one final photograph of it intact before cutting down the middle of the sack from top to bottom with a pair of small metal scissors, lifting it carefully as he went.

Frank had seen many lifeless bodies over the past ten years, but none so grey, so utterly devoid of any memory of life that it seemed as inanimate as the jute sacking that enclosed it. He could clearly see a woman's arm, draped out over the front of her body, over the silt that had washed itself into the bag and found rest inside. An arm so lacking in any colour, he might not have noticed it against the grey sand had he been any further away. The doctor had used a gloved hand to push some of the sand to one side, revealing part of the woman's clothing. At once, Frank had felt both relieved and sad: relieved, because it seemed the woman was not naked, which gave Frank some comfort; although he knew it didn't make her any less dead, and sad, for the life that had once been sanguine enough to wear a red cardigan.

Frank had noticed the priest close his eyes in silence for a moment, before nodding at Dr. McKenna and leaving the room with the undertakers. It had struck him how rehearsed the scene seemed, considering the highly unusual circumstances. But that was priests for you. Rehearsed. Collected. It was impossible to rattle a priest. They were the same no matter how unsettling the situation, how gruesome the find, how stark the realities of a crime scene or a traffic accident. Frank always thought it unnatural. Another reason not to trust them.

'Detective Sergeant?'

Frank jumped. The doctor's head was turned slightly in his direction. Frank approached the table. His nose had been so full of the memory of incense that it hadn't picked up on the acrid, pungent aroma wafting up from the table where the doctor worked, but standing next to him now, it was very evident. Frank made an involuntary gagging noise in his throat, and Dr. McKenna glanced up at him.

'There will be an increasingly strong smell,' he said, looking at Frank with some distaste. 'The remains have been under anaerobic conditions for some time. Exposure to the air is going to result in rapid breakdown of the cellular structure.'

Frank just nodded. He couldn't speak while he was holding his breath, and he certainly couldn't breathe. He noted with awe how the smell and the sight seemed to have such little impact on the doctor.

'I was right to carry out a prelim here. By the time the remains get to Dublin, the degradation is likely to be such that important aspects of the crime may have been lost.'

Frank mustered every ounce of strength within himself and took a deep breath through his shirtsleeve and into his mouth. 'You're convinced of a crime?' He looked from the poor unfortunate on the table below him to the doctor.

'Well, I would have thought the postbag might be clue enough to that.' The derision in the doctor's voice was clearly audible. Frank cursed himself. Of course it was a crime. He knew that. He just couldn't think straight with the smell.

Dr. McKenna said, 'At this stage, it seems clear that the woman's clavicle is broken.' He pointed with a silver instrument towards the woman's neck, or at least, to the place below her head. It was almost impossible to make out any neck at all.

'There is some discolouration not in keeping with that of the rest of the body. And it seems clear, without the certainty of a full PM of course, that the collarbone here', he jabbed at the side of the neck closest to them, 'is misshapen. Broken.'

Frank could see what the doctor was referring to, although it impressed him that he had been able to make it out; the body seemed all broken and discoloured to Frank.

'I'll have to get her up to Dublin.' The doctor kept on talking. Frank could only be certain he was being addressed because there was no one else in the room. 'I'm fairly sure that the bag will be dated to the early Fifties. You'll need confirmation, but I'd be confident of that being an accurate assumption. Her clothes too. It's not certain; of course, we'll need to take samples. She's not wearing any shoes, unfortunately.' He looked up at Frank. 'Shoes are often the best tell in cases such as these.'

He looked back down at the sorry sight on the table before him. 'I'd say she was late teens. Early twenties perhaps.' He sighed again. 'It's hard to guess what she could have done to deserve this end.'

The two men stood in silence for a moment. Sometimes Frank hated being a man. Even after ten years of witnessing the aptitude humans had for cruelty, it still shocked him to think that people could be reduced to such debasement. Because it seemed clear now that this young girl, for that's all she was, had been strangled, put in a postbag, and buried on the shores of the lake.

Frank did a quick calculation. If she had been killed in the Fifties, it was possible that she was put in her shallow grave before the lake was there. She might have been buried in a field that was now part of the lake bed. And if that was the case, it meant Frank suddenly had a very narrow time frame to work with. If either her clothes or the bag gave him an earliest possible date for the girl's demise, the lake gave him the latest. It would be far more likely that he would find a missing person if he knew when to look.

But then Coleman's words from the night before returned to him. So many had left when the dam was built. They hadn't kept track of them all.

He forgot about the smell for a moment. 'What's that?' He leaned over a little to inspect something dark that seemed to be resting on the woman's breast, just under her damaged collarbone. He recoiled when he took a breath, and brought his sleeve to his face again.

'Ah yes.' Dr. McKenna bent and gently poked at the dark line with a blunt-looking scalpel. 'It appears that she is wearing a chain of sorts.' He poked at the chain a little more, until it seemed to come away from the flesh beneath it. With the scalpel and his steel Parker pen, he slowly lifted the length of it until a tinkling noise startled Frank. The doctor lifted the end of the chain, and two heavy looking rectangles of metal dangled from his pen above the woman's chest. For a wild second, Frank thought he saw the woman's black lips move, and his heart leapt inside him.

'Dog tags.' The doctor inclined his head on his shoulder in an effort to read them. 'Well. That should help you with your search for the perpetrator, Detective. Assuming of course that they are not her own. Ha!'

The idea of the poor fragile body before them having served in any army appeared to be highly amusing to the doctor. Frank tried to ignore the impropriety of the man's reaction, and instead attempted to read the metal tags that were still dangling from the Parker pen.

'Here,' he pointed at a box of tissues and Frank handed him one, which he used to wrap the dog tags carefully, holding them in his left hand, while he lifted a small pair of pliers with his right, and cut the chain that held them. He handed the tissue to Frank. 'They'll be of no use forensically, of course. Not having been submerged for any length of time. We'll leave the chain in situ,' he said. 'I'll take a picture of the tags now, and make a note that you have taken custody of them.'

The doctor busied himself laying the tags out on the end of the white sheet and photographing them. Frank's mind raced. He needed to contact his superiors in Dublin. This was clearly no bog body. Something sinister had taken place here and it was now a criminal investigation. He opened his palm to the doctor who set the tags on it carefully. He lifted one up and squinted at it; tarnished with water and time, but the letters embossed on the metal were still clearly visible:

MAXWELL JOHN R

Who was John Maxwell? And what connection had he with the girl lying dead on the table before him? Frank tried to make out the numbers and letters beneath the name, but they made no sense to him. An army serial number, no doubt. Something that would lead them to John R Maxwell. Whether or not it helped him find out what had happened to the girl, remained to be seen. It was of course possible that she had somehow acquired the tags by chance, and had been wearing them simply as jewellery. Lots of people wore weird stuff like that nowadays. But then Frank was fairly certain that young girls in the 1950s hadn't accessorized with imitation army dog tags. Not so soon after the war. No. It was more likely that there was some connection between the girl and John R Maxwell. But where was John R Maxwell now?

There was a knock on the door and it opened slowly to reveal Garda O'Dowd.

'Doctor McKenna, there is a message for you from your office. You're wanted in Crossmolina as soon as possible.'

The young guard stood in the doorway, crinkling his nose. Frank noticed him glance over at the body on the table and avert his eyes just as quickly.

'Right.' The doctor wrapped his instruments in a cloth bag and returned them to his case. 'The hearse will drive her up to Dublin.' He shrugged his camera bag over a shoulder. 'I'll call ahead and let them know to expect her. I'll forward on the PM report as soon as possible. Might be Tuesday at this rate. Detective.'

He nodded at Frank, and turned to leave. What, no goodbye hug? Frank thought to himself. Garda O'Dowd stepped back to allow the doctor past.

'Might you be needing me here, sir?' he looked at Frank, his hand still on the doorknob, his feet still the far side of the threshold.

'The undertakers will be moving her up to Dublin,' Frank said, staring at the metal tags in the palm of his hand. 'Just make sure they get off okay, Michael.' He closed his hand around them and took one last look at the girl lying on the table. He sensed she was listening to him, but instead of being unnerved, he felt somehow reassured. He looked up at Garda O'Dowd. 'I'll see you back at the station later in the afternoon. Right now, there's someone I need to have a chat with.'

TWELVE

The peace that had settled on Casey's Bar that Saturday afternoon was a brittle one. Peggy sat at one of the lounge tables surrounded by a stack of invoices and a stack of delivery notes, trying to reconcile one with the other. Jerome stood with his back to her, his attention on a piece of wood he had leant against the bar. She hadn't exchanged more than two words with him since their earlier conversation, and Peggy had no intention of relenting. She regarded him as he rummaged through their father's old tin toolbox. He had changed his clothes since his arrival, and was now more sombrely dressed in jeans and runners and a plain blue shirt. His Crumm clothes. They certainly contrived to make Jerome blend in more with his surroundings, but his changed appearance made Peggy feel sad. Paisley prints and floral patterns suited Jerome. She thought of how he had looked when he had arrived home earlier, all flamboyance and colour. Now, standing with his shoulders bent over his would-be shelf, he seemed, lacklustre. Deflated.

Peggy slumped back on her stool as she watched her brother grapple with some metal brackets. It wasn't right that Jerome should have to change every time he came home. To have to shrug off his real self and wear the clothes and the demeanour others expected of him. That was no way to live. She stared hard at the back of her brother's head, trying to read what might be going on inside, beneath his glossy black locks. Their mother had loved his hair, even when the others had teased him for its girlish sheen. Her Naoise, she used to call him, with hair like a raven, cheeks the colour of blood, and skin like snow. The most beautiful boy in all of Ireland. Looking back now, it was clear that Jerome had always been the favourite child, not that their mother would ever have admitted it. Peggy wondered what she would have said to Jerome now. She had a feeling that she would have encouraged him to leave Crumm. To stay in Dublin if that was what he really wanted. To live the life he needed to live himself, and not to give two seconds' thought to any Bernie O'Shea or Frances McGowan or anyone else around here who had opinions to the contrary. She missed her mother badly, but Peggy knew the others must miss her too. Maybe she should be more of a mother to Jerome. He had no one else to advise him, that she knew of. And Carla was certainly not one for giving out sisterly or maternal advice. She thought about her mother. What she might do.

'Jerome?'

His name was out of her mouth before she had a plan formulated.

'Huh?' He didn't turn from his task.

Just then, the door opened and a young man in his twenties walked in.

'Miss Casey,' he said when he saw Peggy. 'Ah Jerome. Good to see you, man. It's been a while.' He set a small box down on the bar and shook Jerome's hand. 'I met Carla sunning herself outside.' He tipped his head to the door. 'Having a family reunion, are we?'

'You might be forgiven for thinking that, Paddy,' Peggy said as she walked over to the bar and inspected the contents of the box. She lifted out a cardboard disc, stamped with the name of a beer. 'I'm honoured to have both my siblings in residence today. Although they're both supposed to work here, it's not surprising that you'd be shocked to actually see them doing any work.'

She stuck her tongue out at Jerome who repaid the compliment.

'I wonder why we try to stay away,' Jerome said, holding up the wood and a hammer for them to see. But Peggy saw that he was smiling. 'Kept busy, Paddy?'

'Ah, ya know yerself, Jer … '

'I don't fucking believe you.'

The three of them stopped what they were doing and turned to see Carla stalking in through the bar, the front door crashing open behind her. She was followed by a man, who stalled in the porch, clearly unsure as to whether he should enter or not. Carla stormed past the others as if they weren't there. She went behind the bar and took a bottle of Coke from the shelf, almost breaking it in two at the opener. She stood, swigging from the foaming bottle, staring at the man who was cowering just inside the door.

From his attire and his years, Peggy guessed who this stranger could be. She looked at the fourth finger of his left hand, and there it was, glinting in the afternoon sun shining through the open door behind him. He seemed circumspect for a school principal. Peggy had imagined him all business and bluster, but he seemed shy and subdued. Then again, who wouldn't be subdued under Carla's glare? His slacks and V-necked, sleeveless jumper gave the impression of an ordinary, middle-aged guy. Less Friday-night adulterer, more Saturday-afternoon Daddy. Which, Peggy realized with a sickening feeling, is what he was. His eyes seemed blotchy, like someone who had had a late night. Or been crying. Carla was still standing behind the bar, taking her venom out on the bottle of Coke. She stared over at Tom Devereaux, like a bull sizing up its matador.

Peggy looked at Jerome and Paddy, but they were both still standing with their gobs hanging open. Typical. She'd have to rescue the situation. She turned to Tom.

'Eh, hello. I'm Peggy. Carla's sister.'

The man looked at Peggy as if she had offered him a life ring.

'Hello, Peggy. I'm … '

'Oh, no. Don't even start introducing yourself.' Carla slammed the Coke bottle down on the bar, making all four of them jump, and paced over to where Tom Devereaux was standing. She grabbed him by the hand and pulled him after her, past Peggy and Jerome and a clearly nonplussed Paddy, through the door into the main house. She didn't lift her eyes once to meet her siblings' as she passed. Tom managed to nod quickly at Peggy, but then he was gone. Swallowed up by the main house and whatever fate Carla had for him therein.

'So. That's Carla's new fellah?' Paddy said with raised eyebrows.

Before Peggy had a chance to say anything, the front door opened again to reveal Frank. Peggy glanced up at Jerome, but his eyes betrayed nothing.

'Good afternoon,' Frank said, looking around him as he came in. 'Lovely day out there.'

'It is, Detective Sergeant.' Jerome was the first to answer. 'What can we do for you, sir? Can we get you a drink?'

Peggy held her breath. She stood still as Jerome walked around the bar and proceeded to tidy away the box of beer mats.

'No. No, thank you. I … I was wondering if Peggy mightn't walk down to the lake with me.' He looked at Peggy. 'If you have the time, of course. There are just some questions I have. I could use some local knowledge to help me answer them. If you wouldn't mind.'

Frank glanced at Paddy, and acknowledged him with a quick nod of his head.

'Paddy Delahunt,' Paddy introduced himself. 'Old friend of the family's'.

'Frank Ryan.'

Peggy watched them shake hands. She could hear her heart beating in her ears, and she felt very warm. Frank raised his eyebrows at her.

'Of course, Frank.' She looked up at Jerome, silently willing him not to make a fuss. 'You'll manage for an hour?'

He paused a moment. 'Sure,' he said at last. 'You go on ahead. I'll be grand here.'

Peggy wanted to hug him, but instead she just smiled. As she walked towards the door with Frank, she turned and pointed at the paperwork set out on the table where she had been sitting.

'I'll tidy that up,' Jerome said before she had a chance to speak. Peggy just smiled at him again, and walked through the door Frank held open for her.

'Well,' Paddy swung around and grinned at Jerome. 'If I'd known that there was this much excitement to be had in Casey's on Saturday afternoons, I'd make it my business to be in Crumm every weekend.'

'And you haven't even heard about the dead body yet,' Jerome said with a sigh. 'Sit down there, Paddy. We might as well have a pint.'

THIRTEEN

The way from The Angler's Rest to the shore of the lake was more of a dirt track than a road. Peggy tried covertly to tuck her blouse into her denim skirt as she walked half a step behind Frank all the way down the hill. She smoothed her hair as best she could with the flat of her hands, and silently cursed that she hadn't washed it that morning. The sun was still hot, although the air had definitely cooled a little over the previous few weeks. She watched how Frank seemed to be noticing everything around him as he walked. His left hand was tucked in the back pocket of his jeans, giving the impression of someone in a relaxed frame of mind, but Peggy could tell from the way his eyes scanned their surroundings that this was a man at work. She noticed the blond hairs on his tanned arm. They walked in silence until they came to a fork in the road, and Frank turned to look at her.

'This way?' He pointed to the right.

'Yes.' Peggy thought for a moment. 'Or we can go this way and I can show you the old bog road.'

Frank said nothing; just nodded his head and started on the path to the left. The route almost immediately lost any semblance of a road proper, and soon they were walking side by side on a grassy path through a lightly wooded area. It was cooler here. The sound of branches whispering and swaying filtered down from above them. After a moment or two, the trees cleared, and they found themselves standing on the shore of the lake.

Peggy stopped and waited for Frank to say something. Right out in front of them were two parallel lines of black stumps, no more than ten feet apart. The two lines began at the edge of the wooded area, just a little down from where they stood, and continued on across the silt and into the water, where they disappeared under the lake about fifty feet out. Frank walked out to the nearest stump and put his hands on it.

'This was the bog road into the old village.' Peggy walked over to the stump opposite Frank's. 'These trees once lined the road. I'd only seen them once as a child, years ago, another summer when the water was low.'

Frank stared out into the lake, following the line of the stumps with his eyes.

'I was probably twelve or maybe thirteen. But they were never this obvious before.'

She walked out further to the next tree stump, and examined it with her hands. A rotten piece of wood came away in her grasp. 'I suppose the trees just rotted,' she said. 'Unless they cut them down?'

But Frank didn't answer her. His attention was fixed on something else in the water, further out.

'So that's the mill out there?' he said, shielding his eyes from the sun with his hand.

Peggy followed his gaze. 'It must be,' she said. 'I'm probably not the most helpful person to have out here.' She bit her lower lip. 'I'm afraid I'm like someone living beside the Taj Mahal, but never noticing how beautiful it is. It's always just been the lake to me. And I amn't old enough to remember anything from before the dam was built.' She cast her gaze across from one end of the lake to the other. The sun came from behind a wisp of cloud, making the surface sparkle like glitter. 'Coleman probably is your best bet, you know.'

Frank just smiled at her, but still he said nothing. He stuffed both hands in his pockets and walked a little further along the ghost road.

'Did you used to swim here as kids?' He turned to face her. 'You and Carla? And Jerome?'

Peggy shook her head. 'Not so much.' She walked out a little further before noticing the water starting to ooze around her runners. 'You're not really supposed to swim here. It's not safe.' She laughed. 'I mean, we used to, of course, sometimes. But if they open or close the dam, it can cause underwater currents, so we weren't supposed to. Anyway,' she smiled at him, 'the water's always freezing.'

A wedge of geese flew past suddenly, seemingly out of nowhere, and they both raised their heads at the sound. Peggy watched Frank as he tracked them with his eyes across the lake and over Slieve Mart until they were gone from sight.

'So the body's gone?' she said suddenly.

Frank turned to her. 'Yes.' He indicated with his head, and they started to walk back along the shoreline. 'Dr. McKenna did a preliminary post-mortem this morning. She's gone up to Dublin now. They'll do a full PM on her there.'

Peggy thought about this. 'So do you think it was … ' she stopped.

'I don't know yet for sure,' Frank said.

'But it wasn't natural causes?'

'It would seem not.' Frank slowed his gait until they were walking side by side along the bank. 'Although, we can't be one hundred per cent sure. Not yet.'

Peggy suddenly felt a chill, even under the glare of the three o'clock sun. 'And was she old? I mean, when she was … when she died. Was it an old person?'

Frank just looked at her and shook his head.

'Jaysus.' Peggy thought about this.

Frank seemed to consider something. He sighed. 'It seems she was late teens. Maybe early twenties.'

'Right. Lord.'

'But I'm fairly sure she pre-dates the lake. It's … it's been there a while. I think. At this stage.' Peggy sensed that Frank was trying to reassure her.

'We were just saying', she said, 'how maybe it was a Republican thing? You know? Something to do with the IRA maybe?'

As soon as she had the words spoken, she wished them back. She sounded ridiculous. Frank of all people would have considered that already. He didn't need her pretending to be Miss Marple.

'It's possible,' he said. 'We'll be checking into all missing persons files.' He smiled at her. 'It is possible.'

They continued walking, slowly. Peggy noticed how quiet Frank was being. For someone who wanted questions answered, he wasn't asking too many.

'So do you come across many dead bodies in your work?' she asked.

He laughed. 'One or two,' he said. 'Unfortunately. It's not my favourite part of the job. As you might imagine.'

'Still,' Peggy thought aloud. 'It must be exciting.' She stopped walking suddenly, and pointed to the trees on the bank to their right. 'We used to play at being detectives when we were kids. Myself and Jerome.' She stared into the copse, remembering. 'We would hide behind the trees there, watching the fishermen ready themselves and their boats, pretending they were Russian double agents, off to carry out some dastardly crime.'

Just as she spoke, a car and trailer pulled up in a clearing just ahead. Two men got out and started to untie their little boat.

'You see?' Peggy whispered. 'Russian double agents.' They laughed.

'They don't look very Russian to me, Detective,' Frank said with a serious face.

The two men waved a hello and Peggy waved back.

'You're right. That's Peadar O'Malley. He's a regular at the bar. I'd better leave the investigating to you, Frank.'

They continued walking slowly along the shoreline, past the clearing where Peggy could feel the two men's inquisitive eyes on her and Frank. She could imagine them wondering to each other who that was walking out with the young Casey girl. The air was still, with only the smallest of breezes playing with the tops of the tall evergreens growing along much of the edge of the lake. Behind the trees, sloping fields fell at a sharp incline down to the lake in shades of yellow and green, each field surrounded by a hedgerow, a boundary with its own story to tell. Peggy thought how long it had been since she had walked down here as she did now with Frank. Her mother had liked to take a stroll here until she was no longer able to. Peggy had often held her arm as they had taken 'a turn of the lake', as her mother used to say. But Peggy couldn't recall a time in the last two years when she had walked here. And now, with the warm breeze caressing her face, and the still quiet and enveloping peace around here, she wondered why not.

Frank seemed to be deep inside his own thoughts. They had been walking very slowly. Peggy regarded his profile as he walked ahead of her a little. He had strong-looking shoulders. A man's shoulders. She tried to imagine what he might look like in his uniform. Her stomach burned. She racked her brain for something to say to break the silence that was starting to feel awkward.

'We used to stand on those rocks and throw stones into the water at our feet.' She pointed at a collection of large boulders, which were now easily fifty feet from the edge of the gently lapping lake. She walked over to them and climbed up to the highest one. 'It really is incredible how low the water is now,' she said, almost to herself. In a moment of boldness, she sat down on the flat face of the rock, her feet resting on another beneath it. She thought Frank hesitated a second before joining her.

He sighed as he sat down. 'It really is a beautiful day.'

'Mm hmm.' She could feel her cheeks flush again. She pulled at the hem of her skirt, wishing for the millionth time that she had Carla's legs.

'You get on well together? You and your siblings?'

Peggy looked at Frank to see if this was part of some investigation, but she could imagine no sinister motive to the question. His eyes were trained on the stone building clearly visible in the still waters in the middle of the lake.

'As well as most siblings, I suppose.' She sat up straighter just as Frank leaned back on his elbows and turned his face to the sun. She watched him over her shoulder.

'Myself and Carla can argue. But sure, that's expected of sisters. We were never the pally types. Even though we're the closest in age. Irish twins.' She gave a little nervous laugh, and glanced over her shoulder again at Frank. She couldn't tell if he was listening or not. She thought probably not.

'You seem very different. You and Carla.'

The statement surprised her. Not just because, even with his eyes closed, Frank seemed to be paying attention to her, but because what he said was true.

'We are very different. But hey, she's my sister.' Peggy pulled at a little wild flower that had taken the opportunity to grow up from a crack in the dry rock. 'And she's not all bad.'

Without turning her head, she could tell that Frank was looking at her.

'Her boyfriend is married,' he said.

It was a statement of truth, not a question. Peggy's initial reaction was to defend Carla, but then she realized that Frank didn't seem to be judging her. He was simply stating the facts as he saw them. Occupational hazard, no doubt.

'Well,' she started, 'I don't know if he is her boyfriend exactly.'

Even as the words came out of her mouth she could hear how hollow they sounded. Carla's boyfriend was married. And a father. And her boss. None of which made him an ideal choice. She twisted the flower between her fingers.

'Carla could have anyone she wanted,' she said. 'All the boys always loved her and her long legs and … ' She was about to say her big boobs but stopped herself just in time. 'She never had any trouble getting boyfriends.' She could hear herself defending her sister and she wondered why she bothered. It was unlikely the favour would ever be returned.

'Maybe that's Carla's problem,' Frank said. 'Maybe she needs a man. Not a boy. But it might be better for all involved if he didn't already have a wife.'

Peggy turned. Frank was staring at her with his probing green eyes. She opened her mouth to protest, but his eyes stopped her. And anyway. He was right. Again. Carla did need a man. Someone with enough strength of character to take her on. Someone who could appreciate her good qualities; her thoughtfulness, her quiet consideration, her loyalty. Someone who could knock the corners off her without breaking her in the process.

Peggy saw immediately that Frank was the perfect type for Carla, and her stomach lurched involuntarily. He was the right age, the right position, and he wasn't wearing a ring. He'd phoned someone last night from the bar, but from the little bit Peggy could hear of the conversation, it hadn't sounded like a girlfriend. Not a happy one anyway. But Frank and Carla? Peggy cursed herself for not seeing it before. He had probably asked her to walk to the lake with him so that he could get a better idea of Carla's status. Of course. That made so much sense. All the boys loved Carla. Why hadn't she seen it? She was about to stand up and suggest that they go back to the bar, when Frank spoke.

'My guess is Carla's always going to be a lot of work. A high maintenance girl,' he said with a smile. 'I'd say you know that better than anyone. She'll probably find a nice, quiet teacher or guard to marry, who doesn't mind being controlled by his wife. Believe me, there are plenty of them about.'

Peggy could see with delight that Frank was not including himself in that category. She turned her face back to the lake to hide the smile that had planted itself on her lips.

They sat quietly for a moment. The two men who had parked their trailer in the clearing were now pulling their little boat off across the sand and towards the water. Peggy watched Frank watch them.

'And what about your brothers?' His eyes never left the two men.

'What about them?'

Frank looked at her. 'You get on with them?'

Peggy smiled. 'Oh, everyone gets on with Jerome. He's impossible not to get on with.' She spoke with sincerity, thinking of her brother back at the bar and the troubles he might be going through that no one could help him with. Thinking of him, talking about him, she thought for one awful second that she might cry.

'Does he live in Crumm, so?'

'Yes,' Peggy said. 'Well, no. I mean, yes. Yes. He does.'

Frank raised an eyebrow.

'He does. Live in Crumm,' she said with forced conviction. 'He and I run the bar. Hugo and Carla have full-time jobs. Jerome and I manage the business. That was how it was decided.' She hugged her knees to herself and kept her eyes out on the lake before her.

Frank was silent.

'It's just; he stays up in Dublin a lot. With friends.' She glanced back at Frank. He was still looking at her. She felt a wave of perspiration seep from her skin.

'Is he not happy here in Crumm?'

Peggy's eyes widened. What was with this guy? He'd only known Jerome for two minutes.

'Eh, I don't know. I suppose, I suppose Crumm just doesn't, suit him.'

Frank just frowned and nodded his head. Peggy knew she should stop talking, but she hated awkward silences. And there was something about Frank. She wanted to talk to him. Probably because he actually listened.

'Crumm is a very small place,' she said slowly, 'in every sense. Small place. Small people. And Jerome, well Jerome is a very big personality.'

Frank seemed to consider this.

'It's difficult being different,' he said, after a moment, 'in any walk of life. People like people who fit in. Who conform. But things are changing', he went on, 'and it's easier in Dublin. People are more accepting in Dublin. In cities generally, I think.'

Even in the heat of the sun, Peggy could feel her cheeks burning from the inside out.

'Maybe he is happier in Dublin,' he said, 'but you need him here, of course.'

'I don't need him,' Peggy snapped. She immediately felt sorry and turned to see if she had offended Frank. But his eyes were as soft as ever when they met hers. She swallowed back her ire. 'Sorry.' She smiled at him. 'I studied hotel management. After I left school.'

Frank looked surprised. Interested.

'My plan was to go abroad. For a few years, anyway. Work in one of the big hotels in London, maybe. Or America. For the experience. I thought I might come back after a few years and get a job in Dublin myself. In the Westbury, maybe.' She suddenly felt a bit ridiculous. 'Or, you know.'

'So why are you here?'

The question could have been an innocuous one, but Peggy suspected that Frank was not enquiring about the practicalities of taking over a family business on the death of a father. Why was she still managing The Angler's Rest? Why was she still living in Crumm? Why had she settled? The silence of the lake filled the space all around them.

'It's just one of those things,' she said. 'When Daddy died, the bar was closed for three days. We waked him in the house, and buried him up in Ballyknock. And then, the next day, we were all there together, and someone opened up, and that was it.' She flicked at a fingernail with her thumb. 'I suppose I'd assumed Hugo would stay. Well, everyone had. But the next day, he went back to London, and Carla went back down to Wexford. And, well, that was it. Myself and Jerome stayed.'

'When was that?' Frank asked quietly.

'Two years ago now,' Peggy laughed when she heard herself utter the words.

Frank sat up. 'And you never thought of selling?'

Peggy shook her head, 'It's our home,' she said in a small voice. 'Our parents are dead. What would happen to us all if we had no home to keep us together?'

For a second, Peggy thought Frank might actually answer her question. He had been so insightful up until then, she actually hoped he would. But Frank just looked from Peggy out over the lake, and said nothing. And the reality of her admission became a real living thing. Out there now. Spoken. The truth. Peggy would never sell The Angler's Rest, and her brothers and her sister would never stay. Peggy suddenly felt like someone had slapped her cheek. She clasped her knees tighter to herself. And they sat there, side by side, looking out over the lake, watching the little boat and its two crewmen row off into the distance.

Frank looked at his watch. He should be up at the station by now. Garda O'Dowd was expecting him. And he needed to phone Dublin. His superior officer would be finishing up at six. But it was very peaceful at the lake, talking to Peggy. She was easy to talk to. She impressed him so much: her sense of family, of responsibility. Her sense of duty. And she was undeniably capable. The Angler's Rest was no hole in the wall. She'd obviously used her training to make it the successful business it seemed to be. But then, she was clearly very attached to the place. Very settled in Crumm. She had no apparent yearning to leave. It surprised him a little, but he could see that now.

He could also see thick, dark hair, and soft, pale skin. He knew he had asked her to walk out with him under false pretences. He didn't really think that she could help him with his investigations. He also knew that whatever he was doing, Rose wouldn't like it.

But he was doing it anyway.

He stood up and stretched his arms above his head, looking down on Peggy from above. 'Will we keep walking?' he asked.

They were getting close to the place where the body had been found. Frank could see the old manor house across the lake as the sunlight danced on the windowpanes.

'So Coleman used to be a postman you said?'

Peggy laughed. 'Yeah. It's hard to believe it now. I remember him cycling around on his bike with a big basket up front. That must have been after the dam was built, as he said last night. I didn't know that part of the story.' She looked out over the water. 'You know, it never occurred to me that he might have lost his farm to the lake. I just always assumed he was a sarky old postman who hated children. And dogs.' Some memory made her giggle.

'And he was never married?' Frank said.

'Well now.' Peggy crossed her arms. 'That's an interesting one. I remember my mother telling me once that Coleman had had a girlfriend. Years ago. When he was much younger. Himself and the brother had been considered quite the catch, can you believe that?' She laughed and touched Frank's arm absent-mindedly, as if she was gossiping with a friend. Frank didn't flinch, and Peggy didn't seem to notice. 'Apparently, he had been doing a line with a local girl, when she met some English tourist and went off to London with him.' Peggy bit her lip. 'And that was that. Himself and the brother have lived together as bachelors as long as I've known them.' She looked up at Frank. 'Sad, really.'

Frank thought about this. 'When do you think that was?' he asked. 'When did the lady leave with the Englishman?'

'Oh, I don't know. Years ago,' Peggy said. 'I'm not sure when exactly.' She looked worried for a moment. 'You could ask Coleman,' she said. 'But maybe don't say I told you. I don't want him to think … you know.'

Frank nodded. He needed to check it out. However, if the body travelling up to Dublin at that moment was dated to the Fifties, as Dr. McKenna supposed, it was unlikely to be Coleman's lost love. He would have been at least forty years old back then. Frank couldn't see him wooing a twenty-year-old woman. Then again … he'd have to find her name and check it out. He looked at his watch again. He really needed to get back to the station.

Then he realized where they were and he stopped walking. 'That's the place. Had you seen it?' He pointed to the spot where the body was found, a little farther on. The ground had clearly been disturbed, although someone had made some effort to refill the depression.

'Oh.'

Frank saw a sadness fall over Peggy's features. He watched as she went over to the spot and stood over it like someone might stand over an open grave. He stood next to her and they fell silent for a long moment. With no voices filling the air, he could clearly hear the magpies above their heads, croaking at each other in the swishing trees.

'Poor girl,' Peggy said after a while. 'I hope they find out who she was. What happened to her.' She looked up quickly. 'You,' she smiled. 'I hope you find out.'

Frank nodded, staring into the sand as if some clue might suddenly materialize there. His hand closed around the tissue in his pocket.

'Actually, we did find one clue on the body,' he said. He removed his hand and opened the tissue in front of Peggy. She looked at the metal rectangles glinting in the sunlight.

'What are they?' she asked.

'Dog tags.' Frank lifted them by the top loop and dangled them in front of her. 'Army identification tags.'

'Of course.' Peggy nodded. 'I've never seen them up close.' She put her hand out. 'Can I touch them?'

Frank laid them down on her palm. He noticed the small welts under each of her fingers.

'Wow,' Peggy lifted one of the tags as though it might break. 'So, was she in the army?' Her eyes widened. 'Maybe it was an IRA thing after all?'

Frank almost laughed but swallowed it in time. 'No. We don't believe them to belong to the victim. And I'd be fairly sure that they're not Irish. Look here.' He pointed to the letters embossed on the metal.

Peggy peered at them. 'Maxwell John R,' she read. 'So who was Maxwell John R?'

Frank took the tags from her fingers. He wrapped them in the tissue and put them back deep in his pocket. 'We're looking into that,' he said. 'I gather the name means nothing to you?'

She shook her head. 'No,' she said. 'I don't think I've ever met anyone in the army actually. Ever.'

She seemed almost shocked at the idea. She might be someone who could very capably run a bar, but Frank could see at that moment how innocent of the world Peggy Casey really was.

He tipped his head towards the shore. 'We'd better be getting back. I need to get up to the station.'

'Of course.' Peggy turned to go immediately. They walked towards the small grassy field where Frank had parked his car not much more than twenty-four hours previously. Back before he had ever set foot in The Angler's Rest. Back before he had ever heard of Peggy Casey and her siblings. It struck him as strange how he felt he knew them now. Knew Peggy at any rate.

'So,' he said as he jumped up from the stony lakebed onto the grassy shore. 'Is Peggy short for Margaret?'

Peggy gave a little laugh. 'No, actually,' she said, 'my mother just always said she liked the name. I never really asked her what made her choose it.'

Frank could hear traces of regret in her voice.

'But Peggy Lee was big in the early Fifties,' she said with a smile. 'I'm a bit of a Peggy Lee fan. I like to think I'm named after her.'

Frank laughed aloud, but stopped when he saw Peggy's offended expression. 'It's a lovely name,' he said quickly. 'I'm not laughing at the name. It's just, my mother. She named me after Frank Sinatra. She told me she had to lie and tell the priest

I was named for Saint Francis of Assisi or he wouldn't have baptized me.'

Peggy kept her face trained on the ground as she walked, but Frank could see she was smiling.

'"Nice Work If You Can Get It",' she said, and began to sing, quietly, her voice was creamy and rich.

'Are all the Caseys singers, so?' The question twinkled in his eyes.

'Frank Sinatra and Peggy Lee. That was the only song they ever recorded together,' Peggy explained.

He could see she was blushing. 'Well, if you ever need work, you'd be well able for the stage,' he said. He meant it. An image of Peggy standing behind a microphone in a curvaceous, sparkly dress popped into his head. He coughed. He was glad to see the white walls of The Angler's Rest up ahead of them.

'I'll head on up to the station,' he said as they reached his car.

'Of course.'

'Well, Peggy. Thanks again for your help.'

'I'm not sure that I was any help,' she said, stooping to deadhead some petunias growing in an old iron pan under the windowsill.

'Oh you were, you were.' He opened the door, and noticed Peggy observing it, but she said nothing.

'So, thanks again,' he said.

'You'll be back up to Dublin tonight?'

He thought she sounded a little breathless. 'Probably. Well, it depends on what information I can get from America today. On the tags, you know?'

She nodded.

'Anyway. I'm not sure yet.' He put a foot into the car. 'I'd better get down to Garda O'Dowd now, anyhow. Bye Peggy.' And he sat into the car and turned the key in the ignition.

'Bye, Detective.' He thought he heard her say, and he pulled out a little faster than he really needed to, and off up the road to the village.

FOURTEEN

There was the odd time, the very odd time, when Peggy wished someone from the Irish Tourist Board would happen in on The Angler's Rest in Crumm. When things were good, she knew that Casey's Bar wouldn't look out of place on the pages of any brochure advertising Ireland to American travellers. Were that to happen, it was certain that some of those travellers would find their way to this idyll of an Irish bar, travellers who might otherwise bypass a place like Crumm and spend their dollars in Cashel or Killarney instead.

Tonight was one of those times. As she lifted empty glasses from tables around the room, Peggy could feel a buzz in the atmosphere. It weaved its way through the hum of conversations; a hum punctuated by the odd booming laugh; laughter that would get louder and chatter that would get more animated as the night was oiled by stout and whiskey and bottles of beer. They had finished serving food now, and the last of the empty plates had been cleared to the kitchen. Life and heat danced from the turf fire in the grate, adding to the glow on Peggy's face. Two of the Delaneys had brought a fiddle and a tin whistle in with them, and leather boots tapped subconsciously all around Casey's Bar. Even the smoke rising from fingertips and moving lips seemed to twist and twirl in time with the reel.

Peggy glanced up at the bar where Jerome was busy measuring whiskey into four small glasses lined up in a row. She watched him fill a ceramic jug with water. He looked up at her, and gestured to four men sitting at a low table, their stools turned to face the musicians in the corner of the room, their hands slapping their knees, their feet bouncing off the flagstone floor. Peggy left the empty pint glasses down on the counter. She set the whiskey and water on a tray, and brought it over to the men.

'Ah, would ya look at this,' one of them said. 'What more could a man want after a long day on the lake, but a fine malt served by a beautiful girl.'

As soon as Peggy had left down the tray, the man reached up and pulled her onto his lap, jiggling and dancing her in time to the music. Peggy jerked away from him and stood, pulling at the hem of her skirt.

'Now now, lads,' she said, the smile on her lips never dimming. 'Only food and drinks on offer here at Casey's. Back up to Dublin with ye should ye be looking for anything else.'

She shot a warning glare to the man with the roving hands. As she turned away from the table, she caught Fergal Maher staring at her, his face serious, his fist clenched on the table. She winked at him. Fergal was a good guy. A good friend since their school days. But being the proprietress of a public house came with its own perils and Peggy was well able to handle a few spirited fishermen.

She crossed the room to the fire and gave it a stoke with the poker. She knew she was waiting. Hoping. Twenty times that evening she had jumped when the door had opened, only to reveal someone who wasn't Detective Sergeant Frank Ryan. For the past ten minutes it had remained stubbornly shut. He was still in Crumm. Enda O'Shea had informed her of that before he had taken his pint and sat next to the Delaneys in the corner where he might not be conspicuous in his solitude. The detective would be staying another night in O'Shea's, and would most likely be returning to Dublin tomorrow.

Peggy reached back and tightened the clip in her hair. She felt for her mother's pearl pendant. It was still there, resting against her skin. She didn't usually wear it in the bar: too much of a risk of it falling off, or getting caught in a keg. The clasp was old. Peggy glanced into the copper pot that hung over the mantelpiece, but it offered little by way of reflection. She must get Maura to have a go at it with the Brasso on Monday. She bent down and threw a sod of turf on the fire. Bits of dry straw caked into the peat glowed and fizzled. He was sure to come in this evening. He'd hardly have to work all night. The sound of the front door opening made her start, but it was just Coleman and Doctor, and her heart sank a little. She returned behind the bar as the two men trudged along their well-beaten path towards her. They hoisted themselves up onto the high stools, seemingly ignoring each other as they settled themselves. Coleman threw a battered-looking box of cigarettes on to the counter in front of Peggy.

'Ye'll have to buy yer own drink tonight, gentlemen,' she said with a raised eyebrow.

Coleman scowled at her as he shook a box of matches, which was left on the bar. He turned a little in his seat in order to look at the fiddle player in the corner. Peggy could hear him growling something under his breath. Doctor seemed oblivious to them both. He sat nodding at the musicians as though he was the king on a throne, and they the court entertainment.

'Are we to die of the thirst?' Coleman looked up at Peggy from under wire-brush eyebrows.

She swallowed a retort, and went to pull two pints. Jerome nodded a silent greeting at Coleman and went to open the till.

'No sign of your sergeant this evening?' he said over his shoulder.

'What?' Peggy flipped the tap back with more force than she intended. 'Sure why would he be in here? I'm sure he has better things to be doing with his time than hanging around in bars.' She directed the last part of her tirade at Coleman.

His concern seemed to be focused on the pints she was pulling. 'Go easy on them, child,' he said. 'No pint of stout was ever improved with haste.'

'More haste, less taste,' Jerome said into her ear. She swatted him away.

'Feck off, the lot of you,' she said. 'It would be more in your line to get that thing working, darling brother, and stop annoying me.' She nodded over at the television that hadn't made it out of its cardboard box and was still sitting quietly on the table in the corner.

'Haven't I been trying?' Jerome poured himself a glass of water from the tap, and stood back, surveying the situation. 'I've the brackets and shelf ready. I just need a bit of assistance getting the lot up onto the wall. Hugo can help me tomorrow.'

'Hugo?' Peggy took the coins Coleman had left on the bar and turned to the till. 'What do you mean, Hugo?'

'Oh, he phoned. While you were out swanning around with your detective. He'll be home tomorrow for a few days.'

'He will?'

'Yeah.' At that moment, two girls, a little younger than Peggy, approached the bar, and Jerome turned his attention to them. Peggy watched the blonde one follow every movement Jerome made with her blue eyes, and she watched how he didn't seem to notice.

He finished serving them and turned back to Peggy. 'He rang to say he was coming on Monday, but when he heard about the body, and what Carla's been up to, and your detective … '

Peggy glared at him.

'He said he'd get the first flight tomorrow.' Jerome drank back the rest of the water in his glass. 'I told him we were fine, but he didn't listen.'

Peggy opened herself a bottle of Coke. 'How is it he can just hop on a flight like that? At short notice? He did that before, remember?' She poured the Coke into a glass. 'When Daniel Hogan's mother died, he got a last-minute flight, and was back for the funeral.'

Jerome shrugged. It struck Peggy that he didn't really seem to care either way. Hugo had never been very open about his job in London. He had transferred over there from a job in the civil service in Dublin, but he'd never really told her what it was that he did exactly.

Anyway, she wasn't sure what he thought he was doing, coming back here. Not that he wasn't welcome home anytime. Peggy was usually delighted at the prospect of the four of them being under the same roof. But if he thought she needed him to talk to the Garda for her, or to cope with Carla? Huh. She was well able to handle the lot of them. Hugo had better not start acting like her father, and making her look like a child in front of Frank.

If they ever saw Frank again.

She looked up at the door for the hundredth time that evening just as it opened, but it was only Bernie O'Shea. In for her weekly glass of Dubonnet and gin. Peggy glanced over at Enda O'Shea, smiling and tapping his feet to the music beside him. That smile won't be long on your mug, she thought to herself as she saw Bernie enter and scan the room. Sure enough, no sooner had Enda O'Shea spotted his wife, than he sat upright and wiped the trace of foam from his mouth with the back of his hand. He stood to let her sit, and waved over at Peggy, who took down a stemmed glass and reached for the brown liqueur bottle.

'If Hugo's here, ye could do the flat roof above,' she said to Jerome who was rinsing glasses at the sink.

'We could,' he said. But she knew they wouldn't.

'Another, so?' She looked at Coleman's empty glass. The first usually took him less than two minutes to drain. His pace slowed a little after that. She was halfway through the pull when the foamy liquid spluttered and gasped and the flow stopped.

'I'll get that,' Jerome said and before she had a chance to object, he was gone through the back door out to change the keg.

'Sorry, Coleman,' Peggy said. 'Won't be a minute. Will you last?'

'I'm not drinking the first pint out of a new keg.' He took a cigarette out of the box in front of him, a look of disgust on his face. 'Pour me a bottle there, young wan. You can give some other fool the first pint.'

Peggy didn't even bother arguing, and she reached for a bottle of stout and opened it. She watched Coleman light his cigarette as she tilted the beer into the glass. It was hard not to feel for him. He was still a codger. A borderline alcoholic whose drinking habits were a steady contribution to The Angler's Rest cash flow. But Peggy knew she felt differently about him today. She couldn't help it. She had never thought of him as someone to be pitied, but knowing now, as she did, about his life before the dam had been built, well. It coloured her view of him, of that there was no doubt. He'd obviously had a tough life. She saw now how he might have grown into the bitter, grumbling old man that he was. Something her mother used to say popped into her head. 'He too was someone's blue-eyed baby boy.' She'd said it anytime a beggar had called to the pub, looking for something. And as with many other things, she had been right. Coleman Quirke hadn't been born a crotchety old man. Life had made him that way. The lake had made him that way.

'So were you any help to the Garda, Coleman,' she asked, 'down at the lake? Did Fra … did the Detective ask your opinion on it all?'

Coleman sat back on his stool and exhaled two sickly lungs of smoke over the counter towards Peggy. 'The Detective seems to be managing just fine,' he said. 'He needs no counsel from me.'

'I'm thinking it's Cairbre O'Rourke's child.' Doctor turned towards them, setting the dregs of his pint down on the counter. ''Twas long said he'd put her in the ground somewhere. Little rip that she was.'

He pushed the empty glass closer to Peggy. She ignored it.

'She gave her mother a terrible time of it,' he went on. 'My money'd be on it being the O'Rourke child.'

'Ara blather.' Coleman didn't look up from his glass. 'Isn't that girleen up in Dublin this past thirty years? At Saint Joseph's. She must be forty years of age by now. Still causing trouble from what

I hear.' He half turned to his friend. 'She's no more in the ground than you are yourself.'

Doctor pouted a little. Peggy knew he was after another pint, but she wouldn't pour one until he had left the price of it on the counter first. The back door swung open and Jerome strode in.

'Try that now, Peg,' he said.

Peggy pulled the tap, and after a moment the stout began to flow. She filled a glass and was about to tip the contents into the sink, when she realized that Doctor was eyeing it longingly through slitty eyes. She thought again of her mother.

'Do you want to try this, Doc? See if the keg is good?' She put the pint glass down on a beer mat in front of him. Without a word of thanks he lifted it to his lips and drank half of it back.

'Possibly not the best pint I've had in this establishment,' he said, his eyes shut tightly again. Peggy was about to tell him where he could go to find a better one, when Fergal Maher materialized before her.

'Peggy.' He smiled at her. 'Two pints, please. And a Smithwick's shandy.'

'Taking it easy tonight, Fergal?' Jerome said as he rinsed his hands behind the bar.

'Up to Dublin in the morning,' Fergal said, nodding. 'I've a cousin, plays for the Kerry minor team.' He looked over to where he'd left his two brothers sitting. 'I'm driving the lads up, early doors. Don't want to have a head on me.'

She noticed his cheeks burn a deep red.

'Ah, Kerry'll run away with it,' Jerome said, leaning on the bar. Peggy was about to laugh out loud at her brother's sudden interest in the Gaelic football, but she decided the better of it.

'What do you make of the body down at the lake?' Jerome went on. 'Mad stuff, isn't it? And they think it's a young girl now?'

'Jaysus.' Fergal seemed shocked at this news. He handed some coins to Peggy. 'But it must be there years, no? If it was under the water. It must be all rotted by now? Jaysus.' He shook his head. 'Will they ever find out who it is?'

Jerome shrugged. Fergal took a draft of the shandy.

'They did find some, clues.' Peggy looked from Fergal to her brother. She hesitated, not wanting to say more than she should. But then, if Frank had told her, it could hardly be a secret. 'They found dog tags on her,' she said, hoping she sounded as if she knew what she was talking about. 'On the body. They have a name on them and everything. She was wearing them on a chain. Apparently.'

The two men were wide-eyed at this piece of news.

'No way!'

'Are you serious?'

'No way.' Jerome dismissed Peggy's revelation with the shake of his head.

'I saw them.' Peggy glared at her brother. 'Frank showed them to me.'

Jerome looked at Fergal. 'Frank's the detective on the case. Peggy's new friend.'

Peggy slapped his arm. 'Shut up, Jerome. Anyway,' she finished pulling the two pints for Fergal and placed them in front of him on the counter. 'I did see them. And they did have a name on them. So they'll be able to trace whoever owned them. And hopefully, find out who she was.'

'Wow.' Fergal pushed the three glasses together in a triangle and lifted them in his big, meaty hands. 'That's shockin' awful. Awful.'

'What's that you said, girl?' The three of them turned to see Coleman looking up at Peggy. His face was pale. His forehead was furrowed such that his two wiry eyebrows joined in the middle, almost totally obscuring his eyes.

'What's wrong with you, Coleman?'

'They found tags on the body. Is that what you said? The body at the lake?'

'That's right,' Peggy smiled at Fergal as he stole away from the counter with his drinks.

104

'Dog tags, you said? Like army tags? Metal things?'

'Yes.' She turned to the mirror behind her and straightened her hair-clip. 'Maxwell. That was the name on them I think.'

Coleman sat upright on his stool. He picked up his box of cigarettes and put them down again. Peggy saw him look up at Doctor, but the man seemed to have slipped back into his regular state of semi-consciousness and wasn't paying any attention.

'But it was a young girl, you said?'

'Well, late teens they think. Maybe around my age, it's probably hard to tell. Jerome, will you get the Delaneys two pints before they pass out? Carling.'

Jerome did as he was asked. Peggy walked around the counter to collect some empty glasses. When she returned with them, she noticed that Coleman was still sitting upright, his eyes wide, like someone who had stuck his fingers in an electrical socket.

'You all right, Coleman?' she said. She put her glasses down and touched his sleeve. The cloth felt coarse and dirty beneath her fingertips. 'Coleman?'

Suddenly the old man leaned forward and heaved himself off the stool. He took one last swig from his pint and lifted the packet of cigarettes from where he had thrown them. He lifted his eyes to Peggy's and stared at her for the briefest of moments. Then he turned away and walked out of the pub, pulling his cap from his pocket as he went, and planting it on his head.

Peggy watched him go. She glanced at the clock on the wall. Half-past ten. She had never known a day in Casey's Bar when Coleman Quirke hadn't been one of the last to leave. Doctor suddenly seemed to become aware of his friend's unexpected exit, and he leaned across the bar and took the half-full glass of stout from where Coleman had left it. He held it close to his body and looked around him like a child with a stolen biscuit.

'What did you do to Coleman?' Jerome asked as he passed behind her and reached for the ash bucket.

'Nothing!' Peggy shrugged her shoulders. 'He just stood up and left. He didn't even finish his drink.' She looked over at Doctor, but his attention was back on the musicians.

Jerome took a cloth from the sink and emptied the contents of an ashtray from the counter into the bucket. 'Weird,' he said. As he went to pass in front of Peggy he stopped, and stood for a moment, staring at the pearl hanging around her neck. Then he stood back, taking it all in, her best blouse, her mascara, her tamed hair. Peggy crossed her arms and glared at him.

'Ah, Peggy,' he said with a sigh and went to clean the ashtrays on the tables. Peggy was trying to think of a suitable riposte when the door through to the house opened behind her to reveal a very flush-faced Carla, followed by Tom Devereaux. Peggy's jaw fell open when she saw the smug smile on her sister's face, her fingers entwined in his. Tom's shirt was open at the neck, and his eyes were gleaming. The general glow that seemed to surround them dimmed a little when Carla saw Peggy's face, and she dropped Tom's hand just as they came into the bar. Carla stared straight at her sister. Peggy lowered her eyes and busied herself at the sink.

'Sit down over there,' Carla said in a husky voice. 'I'll bring you over a drink.'

From the corner of her eye, Peggy could see Tom's look of self-satisfaction diminish as he realized he would have to cross from the safety of behind the bar to the very public space on the other side. He nodded in Peggy's direction, but she decided it best to pretend that she hadn't noticed. She stood with her hands in the water washing glasses, only looking up when his back was to her. She saw him scan the room as he made for a table in the far corner. No doubt he felt safe enough this far from home. But still. This was Ireland. You never knew.

Peggy could sense Carla's presence beside her like a rabbit might sense a fox. Her body burned with the indignation she was afraid to verbalize. While she struggled with what to say, Carla pulled a pint of beer. Peggy looked at her sister, standing brazenly behind the taps as if nothing was wrong. As if she hadn't just appeared from the house hand in hand with her married lover. As if her married lover wasn't sitting twenty feet away from them right now, waiting for a post-coital pint of Guinness.

'Don't even start,' Carla said, not lifting her gaze from the drink before her. 'Just mind your own bloody business.'

Peggy's jaw opened involuntarily again, but she closed it with great effort. Her sister's audacity stunned her. She wasn't up to having this conversation with her now. Not here. Not with a full bar.

Their brother, it seemed, felt otherwise, and just at that moment he appeared in front of them, standing next to Doctor, who was still nursing Coleman's pint. He slapped the white plastic tub of cigarette butts and ash down on the bar in front of Carla.

'Are you fecking joking?' His eyes were black, his voice low but threatening. Peggy was a little taken aback. 'You're not sitting here in the bar, with him.' He tossed his glossy black head back in the direction of Tom Devereaux, who was trying to look inconspicuous. 'You can do what you want in the house, but you are not having him and his wedding ring here in the bar for the whole of Crumm to see. Bring those drinks into the kitchen and I'll send your friend in to you, after I've had a little chat with him.'

'Don't you effing dare,' Carla hissed back at him. Her elevated position behind the bar meant she had to lower her face to meet Jerome's. Peggy could see her white knuckles gripping the bar tap.

'It's none of your effing business who I drink with in this bar, or any other. Don't you effing dare try the father act with me. Who the hell do you think you are?'

Peggy stood rooted to the floor, her hands submerged in the suds. She wanted to intervene, but she didn't want to create more of a scene than her siblings were making already. She could see Bernie O'Shea looking at them and over at Tom. Oh she'll be loving this, the auld bitch, Peggy thought.

107

'Get him the fuck out of here.' Jerome's voice was thick with threat.

'Jerome, please,' Peggy whispered. She could hear her own voice break. The Delaneys chose that minute to conclude a set, and the sound level in the room suddenly dropped. Carla opened a bottle of cider and poured it into a glass. Peggy could see her sister's hands shaking. Jerome hadn't moved from where he stood facing her over the counter. And then she sensed Carla's capitulation. She watched her lift the two full glasses and stare straight at Jerome.

'You are such a hypocrite,' she said, her voice shaking. 'Who cares who I'm seeing? It's no one else's business. I'll see whomever I want to see.' She stood up straight and tossed her head so that her long straight locks flicked over her shoulder. Even her hair looked defiant. 'So you can feck off with yourself Jerome Casey. Stay out of my life. And I'll stay out of yours.'

'I'll let your friend know you'll be in the kitchen with those,' Jerome said without a pause.

'No. Don't you fecking go near him. For all I know you … ' She stopped suddenly … Peggy was shocked at the weight of antipathy she could feel radiating from her sister.

'Peggy,' she said, 'tell Tom I'm bringing these out to Ma's old seat in the back garden.' Her eyes flickered over to Peggy and back to her brother. Peggy saw the tears waiting to fall.

'I feel sorry for you,' Carla said, and turned towards the back door. Peggy didn't see Jerome's reaction, for just then a customer came up to the bar to order drinks.

'I'll get those,' Jerome said. His voice sounded normal again, but Peggy was still shaking.

After Carla and Tom's brief appearance in the bar, it seemed to Peggy that the evening took on a different colour. Jerome hardly said another word to her, but served drinks and cleaned glasses in silence, his face dark, his expression sombre. Peggy tiptoed around him, afraid to catch his eye in case he might speak to her with the anger and hostility he had used with their sister. The noise level seemed higher than normal even for a Saturday, and she was getting a headache. She wished the music would stop. It seemed to be making things worse. The four randy fishermen were now standing around the two Delaney boys like gamblers at a cockfight, cheering the musicians on with their whoops and claps and drunken attempts at dancing. One of them tried to get Peggy in a twirl with him, but she pushed him away without any of her usual good humour. She'd give him a kick if he tried it again.

She went behind the bar and pretended to tidy the till. Jerome stood rinsing glasses behind her. His silence was like a presence behind the bar with them. Peggy slammed the till drawer shut and looked up at the clock.

'Will you call time?' she asked. She stood next to Jerome at the sink, challenging him to look at her. He wouldn't.

'I'm going outside. I need some air.'

Jerome glanced up at the clock and back down into the sink. 'Right so,' he said.

When she saw she would get no more from him, she turned and walked through the bar to the front door. A few thirsty customers tried to get her attention as she went out, but for the first time in her life, Peggy Casey flatly ignored them.

FIFTEEN

The quiet of the night outside The Angler's Rest rang in Peggy's ears. She stood totally still for a few moments, her eyes closed, breathing in the crisp, cool air; air blown up from the lake, carrying with it scents of the last cut of hay and the jasmine that her mother had planted in their own back garden. She took deep, cathartic breaths, purging her lungs of the smoke she had been breathing inside all evening. The smoke, the noise, the tension stayed behind her, inside Casey's Bar, and she just stood and allowed the dark cloak of the night outside to wrap itself around her.

She went to sit on the old bench propped up against the wall next to the front door. Her legs tingled with relief when she took her weight off them. If only she could relieve the tension she felt in her heart as easily. She had never seen Carla and Jerome speak to one another like that before. It had upset her. Sure, they'd had their arguments growing up as all siblings had. With only two years between them, it was only natural that they should fight. Sitting there, she could very easily recall plenty of occasions when Carla had turned her attention away from teasing her to teasing her brother who, it occurred to Peggy, had never done much to warrant her ire. She remembered Carla and her friends taunting Jerome about his hair on a regular basis. Jerome had always had beautiful hair. Not unlike herself, Peggy thought, removing the clip and letting it fall around her shoulders. Dark, thick, glossy hair. Carla had most likely just been jealous of it. But sitting on the bench outside of the bar now, she could remember clearly back ten years, could picture the big tree in front of where she now sat, could picture a coven of fourteen-year-old girls sitting on the grass, school bags scattered around them, white shirtsleeves rolled up and white knee-socks rolled down. Girls, becoming aware of the power they could wield, and choosing to wield it on a young Jerome, walking home alone from school, lost in his own teenage thoughts. Peggy tried to remember where she might have been during the encounter. Possibly in the very same place she now sat. And her stomach twisted as she remembered the cruel remarks and vicious rumours given a voice that afternoon. Remembered the embarrassed young man, stoically walking past the gaggle of giggling girls. Enduring. Absorbing.

Now that Peggy thought about it, she realized there had been many such encounters. It wasn't so surprising to her that Carla should treat her brother like that. But something had changed now. Jerome had taken a stand with Carla tonight. And Carla had backed down.

Two years of finding their way in a world without parents had meant that the Casey children had evolved, grown into adults. Their places in life had been shaped. Their places in the family too. Jerome and Peggy may not have chosen to be the ones to continue the family business, but that was what had happened, and this evening had shone a spotlight on the new order of things. Peggy felt a rush of feelings all at once. She saw clearly now what Frank had seen earlier that day down at the lake. This was her life now. Her business; hers and Jerome's. It was no longer their father's place. They were in charge. Theirs were the only important opinions, and they laid the law in the place, even when it came to Carla. Carla had seen this evening that which Frank Ryan had seen within hours of meeting the Caseys. So why had it never occurred to her before? And why did she now suddenly feel so conflicted, sitting out here on the old wooden bench under the anaemic light of the Harp sign fixed to the wall above her?

The sounds of the bar suddenly amplified, and the door swung open beside her.

''Night, Peggy.'

''Night now, Peggy.'

'Goodnight now, lads.' Peggy tipped her head at the two men leaving the bar. 'Safe home.'

The world outside Casey's was quiet again. Was that it? Had she just realized that nothing lay in her future except bidding goodnight to the same old faces every evening, for the rest of her days? That with the satisfaction that came with being in charge of The Angler's Rest public house in Crumm, came the realization that that's all she might be? Ever? That far from visiting exotic cities in distant countries, far from working in plush hotels and an exciting and varied career, she might be stuck in Crumm for the rest of her life, placing orders and totting up ledgers until her long, dark tresses were silver, and there was no one left to remember how she had once been a young girl with dreams and plans outside of Crumm and The Angler's Rest? Peggy couldn't remember a time when her heart felt so heavy. She felt like standing up at that moment and walking away. Leaving Crumm and heading for anywhere else.

But where? She had no one to go to. Her college friends were almost all working abroad now. And anyway, she hadn't been good at staying in touch with any of them when she had moved back to Crumm. And they hadn't stayed in touch with her.

She thought of Frank, and immediately chastised herself. What was she like? Dressing up with kohl eyes and her pearl necklace, pretending to herself that it wasn't on the off chance that he might have appeared tonight. And he hadn't. And why would he have? She'd been fooling herself, thinking there was more to their afternoon walk by the lake than there actually was. What would a man like Frank Ryan see in a girl like her? He had a life and a career and probably a girlfriend in Dublin. She'd been a fool, reading more into his soft tone and probing questions than there was. He was a detective, for God's sake, she thought, chewing her nail. He was supposed to ask questions.

112

Peggy looked down at her hands. The skin on her fingers was dry and rough from washing glasses and shifting kegs. Her nails were in varying stages of bitten and broken. What would any man see in her? Maybe being stuck forever in Crumm was all she deserved. She shoved her hands into her skirt pockets out of sight.

'Tough night?'

She jumped with the fright. Partly because she hadn't heard the man approaching in the darkness, partly because she immediately recognized the strong, assured voice just feet away from where she sat.

Frank.

'Hello.'

Hello. Really? Was that the best she could do? She squeezed the hairclip in her pocket.

'Eh, I'm sure Jerome would serve you inside,' she said. Then she remembered she was talking to a Garda, and she looked at her watch. 'Eh, I mean, you know. If you wanted him to.'

'Relax, Peggy.' Frank smiled at her and walked slowly over to where she sat. The pallid, second-hand light thrown from old sash windows of the bar gave him an almost ghostly appearance. 'I'll leave the after-hours drinking criminality to Garda O'Dowd. I'm sure he hasn't much else for doing. Ordinarily.'

She laughed nervously. 'Yeah. Poor Michael has never been so busy, that's for sure. Although there was the day last June when the Leaving Certificate students built a bonfire out of their school desks down at the bleachers. That had him occupied for a day or two.'

Frank smiled. 'I'll bet it did.' He was standing right next to her now. She had to strain her neck to look up at him.

'May I?' He pointed to the seat next to her on the bench.

She was suddenly very aware of her stomach. 'Of course. Sure. Yes.'

Frank sat down, and the old bench creaked under them both. He leaned back with his legs splayed in front of him. He exuded a confidence she could feel. His hands were clasped in front of him, and he surveyed the darkness before them.

'It's a lovely night,' he said, not taking his eyes off the bushes and trees that separated the front of Casey's Bar from the wilderness and the lake beyond.

'Yes.' Peggy coughed. 'It is.' She was very conscious of the denim-clad leg that was so close to her own bare knee. He was actually here. Sitting next to her. He had come.

'Still busy inside?' Frank glanced back at the bar, and then out in front of him again, as if he really didn't care about anything that might be going on inside.

'Yeah. Saturday night, you know. I had to get out for a breath of air.' She crossed her legs and then uncrossed them again. 'Saturdays are always busy.'

'I remember that,' he said. 'I grew up in a pub too, you know.'

Just then, the door opened, and Jerome's head appeared.

'Are you coming back in or … ' He stopped abruptly.

'Jerome,' Frank said without standing.

'Detective. You're still here? Not gone back up to Dublin?' Jerome came a little further outside and stood sulkily by the door, his arms crossed.

'No,' Frank said, unmoving. 'Still here.'

Jerome looked at Peggy. She wondered if he could see the pleading in her eyes.

'Right,' he said after a moment. 'Well, when you've rested yourself Peggy, you might come inside and help me get these guys moving. Some of the visitors look like they're in for the night.'

But then Peggy saw him hesitate, just for a moment. His eyes flickered from her to Frank and back again.

'You know what? Never mind. I'll manage. Frank.' He nodded quickly at the detective and disappeared back inside the bar without another word.

Peggy smiled to herself. 'No harm in letting him cope now and again,' she said, half to herself, half to Frank. He smiled at her. She shivered.

'So you grew up in a bar you said?'

'Yeah. Are you cold?'

'No.'

She shivered again. Frank looked like he didn't believe her, but he said no more about it.

'My father has a pub in Salthill. He owned it with his brother, but his brother's dead now.'

'Oh.' Peggy suddenly saw Frank in a different light, although she wasn't sure why. 'And you never thought of staying on there? To run it?'

'No.' Frank's response was quick and emphatic. Peggy thought she felt him regret his tone, but neither of them said anything. 'We never lived there. I have a sister,' he said. 'No brothers. We lived a little further out west. I worked there summers and at weekends, of course, but then I joined the guards, and that was that. I was never going to take it on. They never expected me to. Anyway,' he looked at her, 'my father's still in good health. Thank God. He doesn't need me there. He's well able to manage it himself.'

Peggy nodded. As it should be, she thought.

Frank looked off into the distance again. 'Maybe one of my cousins might take it on one day,' he said.

'Not your sister?' Peggy said with a smile.

Frank laughed. 'Oh, no. My sister's not the type.'

He turned slightly towards her, and Peggy thought she might spontaneously combust. Or at least throw up.

'She wouldn't have the temperament for it.'

Peggy knew that she should make some light-hearted comment about his idea of the type of woman who would run a bar, but she didn't want to spoil the moment. Because Frank's tone, and the way his eyes softened when he spoke, made her sure he wasn't being derogatory. Quite the opposite.

They sat in silence for a moment. Peggy imagined him turning suddenly in his seat and putting his arm around her shoulders. She imagined his face right up near hers, his breath on her lips. She imagined him kissing her, his lips strong and firm against hers, his arm pulling her to him, his stubble scratching her cheek. She could almost imagine what it would be like, how he would taste, how she would surrender under his strong embrace.

''Night now, Peggy.' She was startled from her reverie by the three Maher brothers leaving the bar, the two younger ones a little worse for wear. Fergal smiled at Peggy and tipped his head at Frank.

Peggy knew she was blushing. ''Night lads. Enjoy your day tomorrow.'

A few more regulars filed out of the bar, nodding their thanks to Peggy. She wished they'd all either stay or go. She didn't want them disturbing her chance to have Frank to herself. She saw him look at his watch, and clasp his hands together again on his lap.

'Were you busy all evening? Have you finished for the night?' She wanted him to stay here with her. To keep talking to her as he had been.

'Ah yeah. I was waiting on a call back from Washington, actually. They were checking up on the dog tags for me. There's quite a time difference.' He looked at Peggy as if she might not understand.

'Eight hours,' she said.

He looked surprised. 'Yes. Eight hours. Well anyway, they're looking into Mr. Maxwell for me. I was hoping to hear tonight, but looks like it might be the morning now.'

'So they're American?' Peggy asked. 'The dog tags?'

'Yeah.' Frank glanced at her. 'It would appear so.'

'Wow.' Peggy didn't know why it mattered, but she couldn't help thinking how strange it was that the girl had on the tags of an American soldier. She had assumed they had belonged to an Irishman.

'Anyway, I should know more tomorrow.'

'Right.' Peggy examined her fingers again. 'So you'll be here tomorrow?'

'I'll be heading back up to Dublin in the morning.'

'After Mass?'

Frank laughed a little. 'Yeah. Maybe. After Mass.'

Peggy wanted to slap her own face. She could sense that he was about to leave, could almost hear the words coming from his lips, I'd better be off, so goodnight now, Peggy, sorry things haven't, you know, worked out, it's been nice being here with you, but hey, you know how these things go …

'So can I tempt you to a nightcap?'

She heard the words as though someone else had spoken them. She had thought them all right, but she had no recollection of actually asking her brain to send them to her mouth. But they were said now. She might as well go with it.

'I realize it's too late to sell you a drink.' She looked at her watch again. 'But I don't believe there is any law against offering you one free of charge. As a … ' she took a shallow breath, 'as a friend.'

Before Frank had a chance to answer, some more customers exited the bar. Fishermen, visitors to the area unfamiliar to Peggy, who walked past the couple sitting on the bench outside Casey's without even noticing them. She watched them stumble off into the night, arguing about the direction back to their lodgings. Then she stood and looked down at Frank.

'Sure if I'm not imposing,' he said, and Peggy released the breath her lungs had been holding for what felt like several minutes.

'And your brother won't mind?'

'Huh.' Peggy pushed against the door. Something about the familiar weight of it, the feel of the thick layers of paint under her hand, instilled a confidence in her. This was her door. The door to her pub. She had put that last layer of paint there, covering the previous layer that had been put there by her father, obscuring it, superseding it. This was her pub now, and she was inviting her guest in for a drink. And it felt good. 'Of course he won't mind,' she said. And at that moment in time, Peggy didn't care whether Jerome minded or not.

SIXTEEN

Peggy kept her head high as she walked in through the door ahead of Frank, although she could feel the edge of her bravado as she scanned the bar for any reaction to their entrance.

The room had thinned out considerably. The Delaneys were busy putting their musical instruments away, swaddling them like a mother might a child in cotton and felt. Half-finished pints sat on the table next to them. Enda O'Shea sat on a stool just adjacent, silently watching the brothers at their task, an absent-minded smile on his lips, his crossed legs swaying to the memory of music that had ceased. Bernie O'Shea was turned in her seat, clearly gossiping with another woman, but she stopped speaking at the sight of Frank. She laid a hand firmly on her husband's shoulder and drained the glass she was holding. Peggy could guess that she was disgusted with herself for being caught by Frank drinking after closing time. Cow, she thought. She's never in that much of a hurry to leave when it's only me calling time. Peggy took an exaggerated look at the clock on the wall for added impact.

'Goodnight now, Mrs. O'Shea,' she called across the room. Bernie O'Shea's face reddened as she glanced up at Frank who was making his way towards the door leading to the toilet, seemingly oblivious to it all.

118

Peggy went behind the bar and began pulling a pint. She ignored Jerome who had been clearing glasses from tables and was leaving them on the counter before her. Peggy noticed that most of the remaining locals were now standing and draining their glasses. None of them seemed too keen to hang around while there was a detective on the premises.

Frank reappeared, pausing for just a second before approaching the bar and settling himself up on a high stool. Peggy watched without comment as himself and Jerome silently acknowledged each other.

'We could do with you around here every Saturday night,' she said, tipping her head at the door where there was a minor crush of punters leaving. 'I've never seen them so keen to get home.'

'We're not great for business, on the whole.' Frank observed the full glass of stout Peggy left before him. Then almost as an after-thought, he leaned over on the stool and reached into his pocket.

'Oh no,' Peggy said a little too loudly. 'We don't entertain paying customers at this time of night. You're a guest in our home now. No charge.'

She saw Jerome raise his eyes to heaven and shake his head, but she decided to ignore him. Her arms instinctively reached for the empties he had left on the counter, but then she stopped. Sod him. He could clear without her. She did it often enough. She turned and looked at the rows of bottles sitting innocently enough on the shelf in front of the mirror. It was unusual for her to observe them as a customer might, and she rarely drank anyway. But right now, that was what she wanted to do. She wanted to sit and have a drink. With Frank. She wondered for the briefest of moments about the type of girl that Frank usually socialized with. What she might drink. Something more sophisticated than might be found on Casey's shelves, no doubt.

'Too much choice?'

He was looking at her reflection in the mirror.

'Oh, you know. Coals to Newcastle and all that.' She grabbed a glass and held it under the neck of the upturned bottle of Cork Dry. Coals to Newcastle? Did that even make sense?

119

'I'm actually not a big drinker.' She opened and poured a bottle of tonic into her glass. 'It's not a great pastime for a publican.'

She hated the word 'publican'. Why had she used it? Publicans were old men with rolled-up shirtsleeves and comb-overs. Publicans were not modern, self-sufficient women with business plans, and marketing models, and … and menus. She took her drink and walked around to Frank's side of the bar. She sat on a stool next to him, crossing and then uncrossing her legs. Sitting this side of the bar felt odd, and she was unbearably conscious of Jerome's raised eyebrows.

'My father is a card-carrying Pioneer,' Frank said. 'He took his pledge at his confirmation, and he never touched a drop since. He won't even eat my mother's sherry trifle. Although,' he smirked at Peggy, 'I wouldn't eat it and drive a car afterwards either.'

Peggy laughed far too loudly. She took a sip of her drink, feeling the fizz make its way down to her stomach. She also felt the accompanying flush in her cheeks. A good flush. A happy, confident flush. She took another sip.

'No ice and lemon?' he asked.

She looked at her glass in mortification. 'Well, we do, of course, I didn't … '

Frank laughed. 'I'm only teasing. My Da got one of those ice machines. The ones that automatically pop out ice cubes?'

'It's on my list,' she said. 'After the telly.'

'I wouldn't bother. Gets jammed up more often than not. It's more of a hindrance than anything else.'

Peggy nodded, trying to look earnest. In reality, she had just noticed that she could see both of their reflections in the mirror at the back of the bar. She tried to observe them from a third party's perspective. Did they look like two people who might have a drink together? A couple even? She didn't think he looked much older than she was. A little older, sure, but that was a good thing, wasn't it? And although he was sitting facing the bar, his eyes fixed on his emptying glass before him, his body was turned

120

ever so slightly towards her. Yes, if some stranger were to walk in here right now and see them sitting together, there was nothing to suggest that Peggy and Frank were not a couple, enjoying a quiet evening in their local bar.

Although he did look very fair against her dark head of hair. And his tanned, warm skin contrasted strongly to her own pale countenance. Not that her cheeks were pale. Christ, they were the colour of the gin bottle label now, Peggy thought. She pressed her glass against her left cheek, wishing she had put the damned ice-making machine higher on her list of priorities.

Suddenly, her reflection was blocked by Jerome.

'So, you must be kept busy these days in Dublin?' His eyes were fixed on Frank as he rinsed glasses under a running tap. 'I'm surprised they could spare you to attend to something so trifling as a dead body in Crumm. What about all the law-breaking hooligans in Dublin that need corralling and locking up? On a Saturday night? It must be anarchy up there without you?'

Peggy's jaw dropped. Not again. What was he doing?

Frank took a drink from his glass. 'The guards are only interested in arresting genuine lawbreakers,' he said. His tone was flat. Uninterested. Like he had had this argument a thousand times before.

Jerome put down the two glasses he was holding. 'Yes. And you might think, what with all the IRA lads hanging around, making real trouble, that the Garda Síochána would concentrate their resources on real criminals.'

The tap was still running, but Jerome didn't seem to notice. Frank stayed quiet, his eyes focused on his pint glass.

'What would you say, Detective?' Jerome said in a softer tone. 'What would you say if I told you the story of a man, innocently walking home one night past Saint Stephen's Green with a friend, not overly intoxicated, not being noisy or violent in any way, simply walking home after a night out with his friends. What would you say if I told you that an unmarked squad car drove up next to

121

where those two men were innocently walking home, and that one of your colleagues got out, and, without any explanation, shoved that man into the back seat of that unmarked squad car, and drove off with him? His friend was left standing on the footpath with no idea what had happened to the man, until he shows up at their flat the next morning with a black eye and a split lip? And on that very same night, Detective, while your colleagues were busy torturing an innocent man, the IRA were busy abducting and knee-capping some poor fool on the other side of the city. I needn't tell you, sir, what they are capable of. It's no time since they gunned down one of your own in cold blood, in broad daylight. Now tell me, Detective. Wouldn't you say that An Garda Síochána's time might be better spent trying to stop real criminals from committing real crimes, as opposed to exhausting their resources abducting innocent people as they walk home from a night out in town?' He took a step closer to Frank and leaned over the bar towards him. Frank didn't flinch; he kept twisting his glass on the coaster in front of him. 'Well?'

Peggy looked at Frank. She had wanted to throttle Jerome to get him to stop talking, but now she wanted to hear what Frank was going to say. Her brother took a small step back and picked up a dishcloth. Peggy was grateful for the distance created between them.

'That man', Jerome went on, 'had been wearing a gold chain given to him by his mother.' He picked up a glass and started drying it. 'It had a medal of Saint Christopher on it. One of the Garda ripped it from around his neck. It cut him badly. He had to get stitches the next day. No one would dress the wound for him in the station.' He put the glass down gently on a shelf behind him and waved at the two Delaney brothers who were quietly making their way towards the door.

'Night lads. Great session.'

Peggy remained silent, but kept sipping her drink.

'So, Detective. What do you say? Or have you no opinion on it at all? Do you just sit there and hide behind your badge and ignore all that is wrong and evil with your lot?'

Peggy could sense that Jerome was looking at her, but she couldn't meet his eyes. What did he want from her? What did he expect her to do? Join him in his interrogation of Frank, the same man that she had just invited into the pub as her guest, in the hope that they might, what? She didn't really know what. Her glass was empty and she set it down quietly on the bar.

'You say the man was innocent.' Frank's voice was steady. Peggy couldn't help but be impressed at how calm he remained under such an unwarranted tirade from her brother. 'Maybe he was.' He looked up from his glass to meet Jerome's stare. 'But maybe he wasn't.' He sat back on his stool. She saw him notice her empty glass, before leaning onto the counter and standing up.

'I'm not going to stand here and pretend to you that no Garda has ever been guilty of cruelty, Jerome. But it isn't an easy time to be in the guards either. And most of us are just trying to do our job. Uphold the law. We're not all out to get you.'

Jerome just stood there, eyeballing Frank. Peggy sat watching as everything fell apart in front of her.

'Peggy,' Frank lifted his bar stool in under the counter. 'I think it's time I was off. Thank you. For the drink. And … and for all your help.' He tipped his head towards Jerome, and smiled once more at Peggy. 'See you,' he said.

Peggy found she couldn't speak. It was only when he was halfway across the floor that she managed to get the two words 'Bye, Frank' past her lips. Her eyes never left his back until it disappeared out through the front door and out of her life. She was still staring at the inside of the door when the last two customers crept quietly out a moment later. Then Jerome was in her field of vision and she watched as he threw the bolt after them, leaving the two of them alone in the bar. She hadn't realized that she was crying until she saw Jerome stop and stare at her.

'Ah, Peggy,' he said, his voice full of tenderness. 'What is it? Don't cry.'

He went to approach her with open arms, but she sat straight on her stool and put her two hands out to stop him.

'No,' she said, her voice broken with tears. 'Don't come near me. Leave me alone.' She pivoted on the stool until she had her back to her brother, her hands lost in her hair, her elbows resting on the bar. She pushed a full ashtray away from her and held her head in her hands again.

'Peggy. Peggy?'

She could hear him standing at her shoulder.

'Peggy? What is it? What's upsetting you?'

She wondered if her brother could really be so stupid. Could he really not know? He had watched Frank leave, just like her. He had seen him go. Had he not understood? She had thought Frank might be someone … someone special. She had known that he was. They had only talked a couple of times; Christ, she had only met him the previous day. Could that be right? But sometimes you just knew. And he had felt it too, she was certain. He had asked her to walk down to the lake. He had shown up again here this evening, for no obvious reason, other than to see her. They had definitely shared something. He could have been … something. Someone. And now, he was gone. And Jerome had practically chased him out. And he had made it pretty clear that he wasn't welcome back. Oh no, Detective Sergeant Frank Ryan was unlikely ever to return to The Angler's Rest after that episode. Why would he? Why would he bother involving himself with someone whose family were clearly psychotic and irrational? Peggy lifted her head to look at her brother's reflection.

'Are you serious?' she said. 'What's upsetting me? Why did you do that?' Her face crumpled and she started to sob. The sound almost surprised her, but then something within decided that she didn't care, and she gave into it and wept loudly, her tears dripping into little pools on the stained counter top between her elbows.

'Peggy.' Jerome attempted to put his hand on his sister's shoulder, but she shrugged him off. 'Peggy. I'm sorry.'

The note of alarm in his voice only made her cry more loudly. They stayed there like that, Jerome standing helplessly behind his distraught sister, Peggy past caring about the scene she was making. After a moment, she put her hands to her eyes and stopped sobbing. She sniffled and wiped her nose with the back of her hand, before reaching across the counter for the dishcloth that Jerome had been using. She wiped her eyes with it. When her vision was clear, she could see that Jerome was still standing behind her, his face even paler than normal.

'What are you sorry for?' she asked him. 'For Frank? For never seeing that I might have needs, or plans too? For leaving me to cope with everything on my own?' She turned and held her arms out to the empty room with empty glasses and full ashtrays, and a fire almost dead in its grate.

'For this?' she said. 'For this, Jerome?'

'Peggy … '

'No. No. It's been two years now, Jerome. You know, I just realized that today? Two years. What did you expect? What did you all expect? That I would just sit here, every day of every week of every month, keeping things going, placing orders, paying bills, fixing roofs?' Tears started to form in her eyes again, and she brushed them away with the dishcloth. 'Changing bloody light bulbs?' She noticed a slightly bewildered look flicker across Jerome's face, but he said nothing. 'You and Carla and Hugo, you all have your own lives … Carla,' she sniffed loudly; 'I don't even know why Carla bothers coming back each weekend. She doesn't want to be here.' She looked at Jerome. 'She certainly doesn't come back to see me. Her life is in Wexford. Clearly!' She gestured wildly at the door into the house. 'And Hugo,' she paused, 'Hugo's gone. Hugo would have been just as happy for this place to be at the bottom of the lake too.'

'Ah, Peggy.' Jerome pulled over the stool Frank had been sitting on and sat up on it next to her.

'You know that's true, Jerome,' Peggy went on. 'He will never come home to Crumm. Not to live. His life is in England now.

And he has no interest in the business. Sure he had no interest even when he was here.'

Peggy glanced up at Jerome, but he just sat twisting a coaster on the counter.

'And you,' she said.

'I'm here, amn't I?'

'No, Jerome. You're not.' Peggy sighed heavily. After a moment she stood and walked around behind the bar. She took down a glass and held it under the gin bottle again, emptied a bottle of tonic in after it. Then she stood, staring at the space next to the till.

'Lemon.'

'What?' Jerome looked up from his coaster.

'We've no lemon,' she said in a quiet voice. 'Never mind.' She sat back down on her stool. Only five minutes before she had been sitting in the same spot next to Frank, an evening of possibility lying ahead. A whole lifetime of possibility. She swigged from her glass.

'I'll be here more,' Jerome said after some time. 'I said that already. I know I leave you too much. I'll be better.' He reached out and took her hand in his. 'I'll spend more time here.'

For a moment Peggy stopped feeling angry, and only felt sorry for Jerome. She knew he felt no joy in his pledge. His face was full of burden and duty, not excitement or happy anticipation.

'But you won't, Jerome,' she said softly. 'You might try. You might even be around more for the next few weeks, or months. But you don't want to be here either.' She took another swig from her glass. 'None of you do.'

She noticed Jerome watching her drink, but she chose to ignore it. She deserved a bloody drink. Suddenly she was reminded of what had instigated this whole conversation, and she felt the anger rise within her again. She pulled her hand away.

'Why were you so rude to Frank?'

'Ah, Peggy.'

'No. No, Jerome. He had been nothing but pleasant to you. Sure you'd only just met him when you took the head off him earlier. What did he do? What could he have possibly done?'

'Now Peggy. Let's not go there. You really don't want to go there.'

'But I do, Jerome.' She banged her glass down on the counter, noticing that it was already half-empty as she did so. 'I do want to go there. That's exactly what I want to do.' She pushed her hair away from her face to get a clearer view of her brother. 'I liked Frank. I invited him in here this evening. He was my guest. I liked him.' She knew she was repeating herself, but she didn't know how to articulate what she felt. She couldn't admit the truth to Jerome, that she thought she might really like Frank. That Frank might really like her back.

Jerome said nothing, but kept tapping the edge of the coaster on the bar.

'Well?' she said. She reached out and slapped her hand down over his and the coaster. 'And what was that all about? The guy in Dublin? Was that even true?'

Jerome swung around to face her. 'Was it true?' He yanked the collar of his shirt down and tilted his shoulder towards her. A taut, shiny scar ran part of the way around his neck, like a line of red ink on white paper.

Peggy's mouth fell open. 'Jerome,' she whispered, and put her hand up to touch her brother's marred skin. The tears came again. In her mind, Peggy could hear her own questions: when? … what happened, Jerome? … why did they do that to you ? But all that she heard coming from her mouth was her brother's name.

Jerome reached up and took his sister's hand from his neck. He stepped down from his stool, and opened his arms to her and she wrapped herself in his warm, strong embrace, and she wept.

'You're right,' he said after a while. 'I'm not being fair to you.' He ran his hand down Peggy's long dark hair, pushing it gently over her shoulder. 'I'll never come back to Crumm for good. I can't … I can't live here.'

Peggy could hear the honesty breaking him. She turned her head and rested it against his chest.

'I'd like to move to Dublin. To live in Dublin. For good. I should have said it before. I should have said it two years ago.' He looked down at her. 'I haven't been fair', he said, 'to you.'

Peggy wiped her hand across her cheek. She wasn't sure what to say anymore. The hurt of Frank's sudden departure had been muffled somewhat by Jerome's admission. Although he hadn't really admitted anything. But Peggy knew. She had always known. And now she knew how hard life was for Jerome. He felt unloved and unwelcome in his home town, and it seemed that things weren't much easier for him in Dublin either. Dublin; where Peggy had assumed Jerome was totally happy. But where, it seemed, he had been persecuted and vilified. Where life, it now appeared, was every bit as difficult and unforgiving as in Crumm.

But what if he was to stay there? To leave Crumm for good? What if she really was left here alone with just Carla's weekend appearances to look forward to? Carrying on as things were, hoping that another Frank might appear out of nowhere to save her? Was that what she wanted? To be like sleeping beauty, held by the brambles and thorns of Crumm; waiting in a deathlike trance for a prince or a knight in shining armour? And what if Frank had been that knight? What if her chance was gone?

But the alternative – selling The Angler's Rest, leaving Crumm, starting somewhere new – was that what she wanted? For herself and her siblings to be scattered, with no bar, no base, no homestead? Peggy thought of her parents. Were they still living, she wouldn't be in this predicament. Were they still living, she would most likely be in Dublin herself. Or London. Or America. But there was little value in thinking that way. She rubbed her face against Jerome's shirt.

'What do you want to do?' he said, his arms still tight around her. 'Peggy? What do you want to do?

Before she had a chance to think what she really wanted herself, the door behind the bar burst open, and Carla appeared. Her eyes were red, and there were clear lines of black eye make-up running down her cheeks. She stopped when she saw her two siblings in their embrace. She locked teary eyes with Peggy for a moment, before she turned and took a bottle of cider from a shelf.

'What's wrong with you?' she asked, ostensibly to the bottle in her hand.

Peggy pulled away from Jerome. 'Nothing,' she said.

Jerome busied himself lifting stools from the floor onto the tables in readiness for sweeping in the morning. Peggy stood down from her stool, and went to dampen the last embers of the fire.

'It emptied out very quickly,' Carla said, glancing up at the clock.

'There's some benefit to having the guards around,' Jerome muttered.

'Oh, so was lover-boy back?' Carla sneered. 'Maybe you're in with a chance after all, Peg.'

Peggy clutched the iron poker tightly and thought how she'd enjoy giving Carla a good whack with it across her skinny arse. 'I doubt that very much,' she said into the grate. She looked over to where her sister stood behind the bar, one hand on her hip, the other holding a tall glass of cider. The sight of her suddenly made Peggy feel sick. 'So where's your own lover-boy?' she said.

'Fuck off, Peggy.'

'No, no, Carla. You're well able to dish it out. You come home every weekend and dish it out to me. Where is he? Or did you start on him too, and he saw sense? Did he realize that his wife isn't actually half the cow you are after all? Has he gone scuttling back down to Wexford?'

Peggy could tell that Jerome had stopped moving and was standing watching her, a stool turned in his hands, midway between the floor and the tabletop.

'Shut up.' Carla banged her glass down on the bar. 'You don't have a clue what you're talking about. Sure how could you? You wouldn't know a man if he came up and slapped you across the face.' She took a drink from her glass. 'Which is all you deserve.'

'Fuck you, Carla.'

'Right back at ya, little sister.'

'Girls … '

'Oh don't you even start, Jerome,' Carla said. 'You probably ran him out of the place.'

Peggy looked at Jerome. He shook his head.

'Oh yes, is that what happened?' Carla laughed. 'I can see it now. Sure it wouldn't suit our darling brother for you to have any sort of life now Peggy, would it? How could he spend half his time … oh no, more than half his time, up in Dublin, cavorting, or whatever it is you boys call it these days, unless he had you tied down here to The Angler's Rest? Sure it wouldn't suit him at all for poor little Peggy to have a boyfriend in Dublin too. Or Galway, or wherever the hell he was from.' Carla leaned forward on the bar, clearly enjoying the reaction she was getting. Her siblings stood, one by the fire, one by the wall, looking across at each other.

Peggy didn't know what to think. Jerome was still standing, stool in his hands, shaking his head.

'Oh Peggy, it suits us all for you to be stuck here in Crumm till the end of your days. I sure as hell won't do it, and neither will Hugo. And sure aren't you making a grand job of it?'

'It's not true, Peggy.' Jerome didn't take his eyes off her.

'Ah now, Jer. It's probably a little bit true,' Carla said, swigging from her glass.

'Shut up, Carla.' His voice was dark. Menacing. 'You're only happy when you're causing trouble. Trouble here, trouble in Wexford. Trouble for the poor gom wife of that gombeen man. Why are you always causing trouble? You're the same your whole life, Carla. You've never changed.'

'Ara feck off with yourself, Jerome Casey. Like you've never caused any trouble yourself? Don't get me started on you and your little exploits with Sean Hogan.'

'You're such a little bitch, Carla.'

'Stop it!'

Carla and Jerome stopped. Peggy was standing with her eyes shut tight, tears coursing down her cheeks, the poker still tight in her grasp.

'Stop it.' She opened her eyes to them both staring at her. Jerome put the stool back down on the floor.

'Why are you being so horrible?' Her words were almost lost through her sobs.

'Ah for Jaysus' sake,' Carla said under her breath. Then she seemed to notice Peggy's empty glass on the Smithwick's coaster next to her. She picked it up and smelled it, before making a face and leaving it down again.

'Oh Peggy, now I can see what the problem is.' She stood up straight and stretched, as if the whole episode just past had been no more than a boring interlude. 'You know you shouldn't drink gin. How many have you had?' She put her own glass and Peggy's into the sink. 'You don't want to end up like our darling mother now, do you?' she said, turning on the tap and rinsing the glasses.

Peggy opened her mouth and closed it again. She looked from her brother to her sister and back, and then she very deliberately left down the poker against the fireplace, before dropping her gaze to the floor and running behind the bar, past Carla and through the door into the house. She could hear them start to scream at each other as she went into the kitchen, but their voices got lost in the thick stone walls of the bar as she ran upstairs into her room.

SEVENTEEN

Sunday, 28th September 1975

'So nothing back from Washington yet then, sir?'

'Nothing yet, Frank. We did have a little bit of luck though.'

'Sir?'

'Hugo Casey. The brother of the family helping you with your investigation? Turns out he works in the embassy in London.'

'He does?' Frank was surprised at this revelation. Peggy hadn't mentioned Hugo worked in the embassy.

'Yes. One of the lads here recognized the name. Anyway, he put in a call for us last night, to one of his colleagues in Washington. It might help, you know, speed things along a little.'

'I see. But nothing back from them as yet?'

He could hear his superior officer bristle a little all the way up in Dublin.

'It is Sunday you know, Frank. It's bound to take a little longer than usual. Not enjoying your weekend break then? Anxious to get out of the sticks, are we?'

'No, of course not, sir.' Frank glanced over at Garda O'Dowd seated at the only other desk in the little station room. 'It's just; well it would obviously help a lot. With the investigation. Specifically with the timing of the victim's demise.'

'Are you getting anywhere with the locals?'

Frank leaned back in his chair. 'There is one man here. He … he has raised some suspicions. Nothing concrete, but I would like to question him again.'

'This, Coleman Quirke man you mentioned?'

'Yes, sir.'

'No one else?'

Frank leaned in over the desk. 'Well until I have a date on the body or a lead on the dog tags, sir … '

'Yes, yes. All right Frank. I get it. Look as soon as we have anything, I'll get on to you there.'

'Right, sir.'

'And don't worry, Frank. We won't abandon you in Crumm. If it comes to it, I'll send some good men in to get you out.'

Frank could hear the older man chuckle at his own joke before a loud click told him that he had hung up his receiver. Frank replaced his own handset and leaned heavily on the desk.

'Everything all right, sir?'

Frank looked up to see Garda O'Dowd watching him.

'No leads on the tags so, sir?'

'Not yet, Michael.' Frank picked up a pencil and tapped it on the arm of his chair. The space was cramped with the two desks in it. He guessed the second one had been dragged in from some other place for Frank's own use. Frank didn't envy Garda O'Dowd his working conditions. It was obvious that the building had never been meant for use as a Garda Station. Two small sash windows leached what little light they could into the room, not helped by the half net curtains suspended across each; curtains that looked like they could do with a good wash.

'Did you know that Hugo Casey worked for the Irish embassy in London, Michael?'

Garda O'Dowd stood and went over to a small kitchen unit in the corner of the room to a shiny electric kettle. 'I didn't, sir,' he said, flipping the red switch. 'But then I can only say that I have met the man once or maybe twice in my time in Crumm.' He turned to look at Frank. 'He'd rarely be here, sir. I knew he worked in London all right. He seems not to be too interested in visiting his home place. To my knowledge, sir.'

Frank nodded his head and leaned back into his wooden chair. 'And how long have you been stationed in Crumm, Michael?'

Garda O' Dowd turned and took two mugs from a shelf. 'Just eighteen months, sir,' he said, putting two spoons of tea from a packet into a small brown teapot.

'Your first posting?'

'Sir.'

Frank thought about the decision to put a rookie guard into a one-man station in the middle of nowhere. He guessed Michael must not have any relations with any pull in the force. That, or he had done something to annoy one of his training officers.

'Your father a guard?' he asked.

'No, sir.' Michael stirred the pot and poured two mugs of tea. He brought one over to Frank's desk, and left a small bottle of milk down beside it. 'My father died when I was sixteen. It's just my mother. And I've five younger sisters, all still at school.'

'I see.'

Michael turned away from him. Frank watched as he put three sugars into his own mug of tea before turning back around to face him. 'They rely on me, of course,' he said.

'Of course.' Frank considered Garda O'Dowd. In an instant he had gone from being the young local guard, still wet behind the ears and a source of comedy for the locals, to being the sole provider for a large young family. He watched him slurp his tea, his tall frame hunched over as if the ceiling might be too low to fit him. He wondered if the other people in Crumm knew about his family. He wondered if Peggy knew.

'So you'd like to question Coleman Quirke, sir?' Michael nodded his head towards the phone on Frank's desk.

'I think so. I mean, yes.' Frank tried to refocus on the case. 'I'm not convinced that he has done anything wrong now,' he said. 'I just think it would be worth bringing him in. Asking him a few questions.'

'Right so, sir. Will I go over to his place now? See if he's there?'

Frank looked at his watch. It wasn't yet nine. 'It's still very early. Let's give Dublin Castle a couple more hours. See if they have heard anything back from Washington. A lead on the dog tags could be very helpful.' Frank swallowed a mouthful of his tea. 'Coleman Quirke isn't going anywhere.'

EIGHTEEN

'And the national school's cake sale after Mass last Sunday raised twelve pounds for the black babies in Africa. Well done, girls. Although, I might ask that you don't do it too often.' Father Francis patted his belly. 'I'm going to have trouble fitting into my Christmas vestments at this rate.'

Peggy rolled her eyes while polite laughter broke out around her. Across the aisle, the national school's principal was grinning like a fool.

'Wednesday evening will be the annual whist night in Our Lady's hall. This year we are raising money for Mrs. O'Shaughnessy's new wheelchair, a most worthy cause, I'm sure you will agree. And,' he looked up from his notes, 'I might repeat that, should anyone have any information as to what might have happened to Mrs. O'Shaughnessy's first wheelchair, they speak to me at any time, in confidence. Indeed,' he said, 'I find that the confessional box is a very suitable place for such, confidences. So,' he went on, 'I'll leave it at that. But remember,' he added, apparently unable to leave it at that, 'Mrs. O'Shaughnessy has been without a chair for six weeks now, and unable to attend the bridge for as many weeks as a result.'

The usually cool church had been warmed by a summer of unbroken sunshine, and Peggy found herself starting to doze off.

She was being propped up by shoulders on either side, so full were the pews. And she hadn't slept much.

'And anyone who has not put their name on the list for the bus to Knock, could they do so today please. A place cannot be guaranteed if your name is not on the list.'

Peggy's eyelids were gradually falling. She could just about make out the back of Martina Griffin in the pew in front of her. She noticed how nice her plait was, roped around her head in a way Peggy had seen done in a magazine. As she dozed she thought how maybe there was another person who read fashion magazines in Crumm after all. She could hear Father Francis droning on in the background.

'Finally, today, I want you to join me in a special prayer. Perhaps we might kneel.'

Peggy jolted awake as the two warm bodies either side of her were suddenly no longer supporting her weight. All around her, the faithful were on their kneelers, heads bowed. Peggy followed their lead, a little disoriented. For a moment, she thought she had slept through the whole consecration.

'As many of you will know, the body of a young woman was found on the shores of the lake, only a few short days ago. She has since been removed to Dublin. Now, whereas we pray that there was no devilry at play, it does seem at this stage that it might have been some evil-doing that resulted in this … ,' he looked up at the congregation, 'this tragedy. And so', he bowed his head, 'let us take a moment in silence to pray for the soul of our sister. And on this eve of the feast days of Saints Michael and Gabriel and Raphael, archangels of the Lord, let us pray that our sister might at last receive a proper Christian burial, and that these, most holy angels of the Lord, might see her safely, at last, to the gates of heaven.'

The priest paused, and Peggy noticed many heads bow in silent prayer for this person whom they had never known. She too dropped her forehead to her hands, but her mind turned straight to Frank.

'And may the Lord guide the Gardaí and those tasked with finding out the truth about our poor unfortunate sister.'

Peggy held her breath as the whole town prayed for Frank around her. She wondered if he was present, and she lifted her head to look towards the back of the church. As was customary, many of the men of the village stood there. She scanned their faces, searching, hoping, but he wasn't amongst them. As she turned back, she caught Carla's eye: Carla, who had not been up in time to walk to Mass with her as was their usual Sunday routine. She must have come late, Peggy thought. She was sitting closer to the rear. It surprised her to see what seemed like a genuine smile on her sister's face. A smile perhaps tinged with apology. Peggy looked away. Then it struck her that she had not seen Coleman standing at the back of the church either. She turned again, and looked at the water font, where she and all her siblings had been baptized. That was his usual spot. It was there that Coleman could be found most Sunday mornings, grunting and muttering his way through Mass until Holy Communion, when he would be gone as fast as his bockety old legs would carry him.

Something made Peggy feel uneasy. It was highly unusual for Coleman not to be standing there. Unless he had somehow acquired a ticket for Croke Park and was already on the road up to Dublin to see the game with the rest of them. He might have got a lift with the Maher brothers. Not many would have taken him with them, but Fergal would have.

But no, Peggy knew that it was a very unlikely scenario. She thought of how he had left the bar so abruptly the previous night. Now that she had the opportunity to dwell on it, she could see how really strange that had been. Someone must have said something to him. Or what if he were sick? Peggy started to worry. She wondered if Coleman had made it home at all. His brother wasn't here, from what she could tell, but he never came to Mass unless there was a funeral, and even then he rarely crossed the threshold. What if Coleman had been feeling unwell? What if that was why he had left the bar? What if he had had a heart attack or something on his way home? She was fairly certain that the two brothers didn't have a phone in the house. Desmond might not have noticed that his brother was missing until this morning, and even then might not have noticed.

Peggy felt very claustrophobic all of a sudden. She sat and knelt with the rest of the people in the pew, but she heard very little of what the priest said, and she certainly said no prayers herself. As she stood to join the line filing up to receive Holy Communion, she considered turning right instead of left and leaving with the others who took this part of the proceedings as their cue for joining the exodus. But then she reconsidered. She was probably overreacting. She'd get Jerome to drive over to the old man's cottage after Mass, just to check in on them. In all likelihood, Coleman was fine.

'There's a rumour going around that ye might be showing the match in Casey's?'

The whisper came from behind her left ear. She was only three people away from Father Francis in line, however, so she couldn't turn her head to see who was speaking.

'In colour?' the voice said.

'Body of Christ.' The priest waited for Peggy to stick out her tongue. 'Amen.'

On her way back to her seat, Peggy turned and saw Jim Coneeley's balding head bent over as the priest reached up to give him his Communion. As she squeezed her way into her pew, she saw that Carla was sitting in her place, staring straight ahead of her. Peggy knelt next to her for a moment, more out of habit than intent. She couldn't clear her mind enough to pray anyway, and it felt disingenuous praying that Frank Ryan would somehow need to return to The Angler's Rest one more time before leaving for Dublin. So after a moment, she sat back beside Carla. Their shoulders were touching. Neither of them said anything. They watched the priest finish his ablutions on the altar.

'I hear the match is being shown in Casey's this afternoon?' A gravelly voice breathed foul-smelling air into Peggy's ear. Before she had a chance to reply, Carla twisted slightly in her seat and leaned back towards the source of the query.

'It would be more in your line to be saying your prayers, Joseph McGowan,' she said.

Even her whisper could cut you dead, Peggy thought, impressed.

'I'd be praying no one tells the priest that they saw yourself and one of the Hogans having races down the main street in auld Ma O'Shaughnessy's wheelchair after fifteen pints between ye at Grogan's.'

Peggy sniggered loudly, and felt the removal of the foul air from her shoulder. She caught Carla's eye and her sister winked at her.

'Let us pray,' the priest said from the pulpit, and the two Casey sisters knelt side by side.

Outside the church, the talk for the most part seemed to be about the body found at the lake. That, and whether or not Kerry could pull off the double later that day in Croke Park. The two Caseys hurried past the hand-shaking priest and walked off down Crumm main street, past the little houses and shops. Every door was shut, excepting McGowan's, which was open to sell the papers. They walked just out of the town, as far as the right turn down towards the lake, without a word passing between them.

'Your sign could do with a lick of paint,' Carla said as they turned off the main road, passing the ridiculously large wooden hoarding that advertised The Angler's Rest.

'It's as much your sign as my sign.'

Carla chuckled. 'I'm sorry about last night. About what I said,' she glanced sideways at Peggy as they walked. 'No one wants you to be miserable here,' she went on. 'If you ever wanted to leave, well, we'd just have to cope.'

Peggy wasn't sure which she was more shocked at – her sister's belligerence the evening before – or the quiet compassion she was showing to her now.

140

'I'm leaving, Peggy,' she said.

'What?' Peggy stopped walking. 'What do you mean you're leaving? Leaving where?' She watched Carla's back as she kept walking on down the hill. 'Carla?'

Carla stopped and turned. 'It's not working out,' she said. She stood there, drawing circles in the gravelly path with her runner. Peggy thought how young she looked, her hair pulled into two, thin pigtails over either shoulder, her long legs stretching out from beneath her grey corduroy skirt. She could have been seventeen, from a distance. Up closer, whatever demons Carla struggled with made her look all of her twenty-four years. The eyes don't lie.

'With Tom,' she said at last. 'It's not working out.' She crossed her arms and stood up straight. 'Look, Peggy, I think we all know it was never going to work out. Maybe I thought it might have. Once.' She turned her eyes sharply on her sister. 'He really isn't happy at home, you know.'

Peggy started walking slowly towards her. They continued together on the path towards their home.

'So,' Peggy said, 'where are you going?'

'Australia. Sydney. I think.'

'What?' Peggy stopped for the second time. 'Australia? What are you talking about? Why would you go to Australia?'

A middle-aged man walked past them, the Sunday paper under his arm, a pint of milk in his hand.

'Girls.'

'Hello, Tommy,' Peggy said, distractedly. She waited until the man was a good way ahead before she spoke again.

'Australia, Carla? Are you serious? Who do we know in Australia?'

'No one,' Carla said. 'That's exactly the point, sister dear. And they're looking for teachers over there. And the pay is good.' A breeze blew up the road from the lake, and she crossed her arms again. 'Better than here, anyway.'

'But Australia?' Peggy was torn. Last night she would have gladly seen her sister sail off into the sunset to Timbuktu. She would have bought her the ticket herself. But as was always the way with Carla, when it came to it, she couldn't stay angry with her. She was blood. And that's all there was to it.

'So you see; I won't be here anymore. At weekends. Not from Halloween anyway. The school year starts there in January. I'll probably have to leave next month.' She pulled at her pigtails. 'I haven't all the details worked out yet.' She looked over at Peggy walking beside her. 'Not that I've been much help to you anyway,' she said. 'I know that.'

Peggy didn't know what to say. They were almost at home now. She could see someone had turned on the lanterns either side of the front door, even though the day was bright. Probably Maura. She was always knocking against the switch with her duster.

'I told Jerome last night,' Carla said. 'Peggy.' She pulled her sister by her hand so that they were facing each other. Without heels, Peggy's eyes were just in line with Carla's chin. 'I'm not asking you to stay here. Of course, I'd hate ... I'd hate for the place to be sold.'

She turned and looked up at the gable wall of the pub, the flowers in their window boxes, the Harp sign hanging over the old rickety bench, the lanterns either side of the painted door. Behind it, their home, sheltered by the bar, irrevocably connected to it, just as their family's life within those walls had been.

Peggy couldn't imagine selling the place. She couldn't contemplate driving past some day, and seeing someone else running the business there, raising a family in the house. It was the Caseys' business. The Caseys' home.

And yet, the Caseys were all but gone. None of them wanted to be here. None but herself, and she wasn't even sure if she wanted it either.

'You know, you really have made a great go of it,' Carla said, her gaze fixed on the sign above the door: The Angler's Rest, prop. Patrick M. Casey & Son. 'You never changed it.'

Peggy looked at the painted wooden sign. 'No.' She remembered the day her father had fixed it to the wall. Before Hugo had left for Dublin. The summer after his Leaving Certificate, when her father had made the assumption that that was how it would be.

Patrick M. Casey & Son.

'Come on,' Carla linked arms with her sister. 'Let's go in. Hugo might be back by now.'

NINETEEN

Inside The Angler's Rest, the two Casey brothers were standing, one on a stepladder, the other balancing precariously on a table, their backs to their two sisters as they entered. Hugo seemed to be holding Jerome's homemade shelf aloft, while Jerome was expending great effort turning a screwdriver into a bracket beneath it.

'Oh, God bless the work,' Carla said.

'I told them they'd be better off getting Mick O'Leary to do it.'

Peggy turned to see Maura sitting on one of the stools in the window, a mug of tea and a newspaper on the table in front of her. Carla went and stood beside her, draping her arm across Maura's shoulder, reading the headlines over her head.

'Sure he'd have it done in half the time. Doesn't he have all the right equipment and what not. A drill,' Maura went on, 'an electric drill is what they need.' She turned her attention back to her newspaper. 'And then I wouldn't be scared out of my wits walking under it every day,' she grumbled into her tea. 'Expecting it to fall on my bloody head.'

'Maura, Maura, Maura. Have you no faith?' Jerome jumped down and lifted the heavy television set into his arms. 'Wait till you see,' he panted with the exertion. 'It'll be fabulous. Well, girls?'

144

Hugo turned to look over his shoulder at his sisters. 'Hi Peggy,' he said. 'Carla.'

'Hugo,' Carla said, and she left Maura to her paper and disappeared behind the bar and through to the house beyond.

'Lovely to see you too,' Hugo muttered, turning his attention back to the shelf. 'How are you Peggy?'

'Tired,' she answered, sitting down next to Maura at the little table. 'Although you must be too. That must have been an early start for you.' She drummed her fingers on the table. 'What has you rushing home so urgently? Were you worried that the television wouldn't find its way up onto the wall without you?' She could sense Maura's silent surprise at her tone.

'I was due to be in Dublin tomorrow anyway,' Hugo said. If he had heard the accusation in Peggy's voice, he didn't let on. 'I got the chance of a seat on the dawn flight today, so I took it. A few of the lads from the office were coming back today. For the match. So I travelled with them.'

'Right.' Peggy relented. 'Well, it's nice to see you. It's been … it's been an eventful few days in Crumm. I'm sure Jerome has been filling you in.'

'Right. That should do it.' Jerome jumped down from the table he had been balancing on, and stood back to admire his work.

Hugo tentatively removed his hands from the shelf. It didn't fall. He pulled at it a little. It seemed secure. 'Not bad, Jer,' he said.

Peggy watched him from across the room as he cautiously descended the stepladder. She noticed how his shirt bulged over his trouser belt. Standing next to Jerome, there were obvious similarities, but somehow, Hugo looked like a less shiny, less polished version of his younger brother. They were a similar height, but Hugo was a rounder, more homely version of the slim, fresh-faced Jerome. His hair was thicker too, and cut shorter. But when he turned to look at Peggy, she saw the same sparkling blue eyes, and any negative thoughts towards her older brother dissipated.

Hugo brushed his hands off each other and came over to sit next to Peggy and Maura.

'Are you hungry?' she asked him.

'Nah. I'll get something in a while. I had a breakfast on the plane.'

'Imagine that,' Maura said, shaking her head.

'So how are you?'

'Me?' Peggy sat back. 'I'm fine. What would be wrong with me?' She glanced up at Jerome, who seemed very taken with the instruction booklet that came with the television.

'Well, Jerome mentioned … I hear Carla was causing ructions. Again.'

Peggy examined her fingernails. 'Jerome is well able to cause ructions himself,' she said.

'Hey!' Jerome lifted his head from the booklet.

Hugo ran his finger over the wooden tabletop. 'And how's business?'

Peggy's stare narrowed on her oldest brother. 'Business is fine. What's this about, Hugo? What has Jerome been saying to you?'

'Nothing, nothing.' Hugo looked over at his brother but any assistance he was expecting was clearly not forthcoming. 'Nothing. I suppose … I suppose we just thought that maybe we should have a talk. About the pub. About … about the future.'

Peggy felt herself starting to panic a little. She looked from Maura to Hugo, and over to Jerome. 'Why is this all coming up now?' she asked. 'Is this why you are home, Hugo? Had you all this planned? Do you want to sell, and you were afraid to tell me?'

Maura's mouth fell open. 'Is that true, Hugo?' she said, horrified. 'You can't want her to sell The Angler's Rest?'

'No … ' Hugo started.

'And after all the work she's put into it over the past two years.'

'Maura, we're not … '

'Sure if it wasn't for Peggy, this place would be just another hole in the ground, like … like … like Grogan's. You may not remember, Hugo Casey, nor you, Jerome, but things were not good here after your mother died. This place very nearly closed on more than one occasion.'

None of them spoke then. Peggy was surprised. She hadn't known that The Angler's Rest had been in trouble.

'If it wasn't for Peggy and her ideas,' Maura went on, 'well. Well you wouldn't have anything to sell, Hugo Casey. And God knows where you'd all be if she hadn't kept the lot of you together.'

Maura started to get weepy, and Peggy reached over and patted her arm.

'Maura.'

'No. It's true. You have been the centre of this family for the past two years, Peggy. If it weren't for you, sure … sure I'd never see any of you.' She took a crumpled tissue from inside her sleeve and wiped her nose with it. 'And I suppose Carla has told you she is going.' She dabbed at her eyes.

The lack of surprise on Hugo's face told Peggy that he already knew about Carla. Jerome must have told him. Or maybe he had known for weeks. Maybe they had all known but herself.

'So you can't sell the place from under her,' Maura said. 'You just can't.'

'Maura,' Hugo said quietly. 'No one will sell The Angler's Rest unless everyone wants to sell it. It's Peggy's home. As long as she wants it to be. I … we just thought that perhaps she might want to … to move on.' He glanced up at Peggy. 'She might not want to spend the rest of her life here either. And so maybe it's a good time to start thinking about it. Just, thinking about it.'

Maura sniffed loudly. Peggy noticed that Jerome has stopped pretending to read the television instructions and was leaning back against the bar on his elbows.

Forty-eight hours ago she had been preparing for another run-of-the-mill weekend in Crumm. She had never heard of Detective Sergeant Frank Ryan, or met Tom Devereaux, or known about Carla's plan to emigrate to the other side of the world. She hadn't expected to go walking by the lake with a man she had just met, or to learn about the awful things that Jerome had been enduring in Dublin. And she had certainly not expected to be sitting here, contemplating the sale of The Angler's Rest. Forty-eight hours ago, she had been placing keg orders, planning to tar the roof, thinking about getting the front wall repainted, choosing which tile to put behind the sink.

Now ... now she was suddenly faced with a whole new choice. The choice of a new beginning. A new life. She could go anywhere. If they sold the pub and the house, she'd have enough money to make a proper start somewhere else. To work in a real hotel. In Dublin maybe, or London. Or Boston.

Peggy saw three faces staring back at her. Were they really going to give her this opportunity? Just when she thought she was stuck forever in her father's bar in Crumm, were they really offering her the chance to break free? And did she want to take it?

The silence was thick in the room. It mixed with the previous night's turf and smoke fumes. A shard of sun sliced through the window next to Peggy, and she watched as the dust motes danced in the air above the table in front of her. Then the silence was broken by the sound of the front door opening, and a low, growly moan. The four of them turned to see Coleman stumble in the door.

'Coleman!' Peggy jumped up from her seat, flushed with guilt. She had forgotten all about Coleman.

Hugo, who had no reason to be concerned for the man, just stood and went behind the bar. 'Coleman,' he said. 'You're earlier than usual, sir. I'm not sure that we're even open yet.'

Coleman hadn't moved from the little porch inside the door, and he stood, leaning against the archway into the bar, a wilder look than usual in his eyes.

'Coleman.' Peggy went over to him. 'Are you okay? I didn't see you at Mass. I was beginning to worry.' She heard Maura tut-tutting to herself. Peggy knew the others wouldn't understand, but she was so relieved to see the old man standing there, that she didn't care. 'Will I get you a drink?' she asked him, gesturing to the bar.

Coleman made a noise, somewhere between a cough and a growl. 'And I'm not here for the drink,' he said. Peggy caught the look of surprise on Maura's face.

'Arrgh.' Coleman tugged at the rope holding up his trousers. 'I need … I need … ' He pointed wildly to the door leading out the back to the toilet. After a second, he pushed past Peggy and half-walked, half-dragged himself across the room and disappeared behind it.

Peggy stood at the porch, her mouth open. 'What's wrong with him?' she said to her two brothers. But neither of them seemed to have taken any notice. Jerome's head was back in the white pages of the booklet.

'Did you not think he looked awful?' Peggy said to Maura.

'More than usual?'

'Yes. Yes, more than usual.'

Maura shrugged.

Peggy threw her a dirty look. 'Jerome,' she said.

'Hmm?' Jerome turned a page of the booklet.

'Jerome,' Peggy persisted. 'Go on after him and make sure he's all right. What if he's having a heart attack or something?'

Jerome looked at Peggy as if she might be as mad as Coleman herself. 'What's got into you?' he said. 'There's not a thing wrong with him. He'll be back out in a minute. Leave the man alone.'

Then Peggy heard a noise directly behind her, and she turned to see Garda O'Dowd coming in the door. He almost stood on her in the porch, and she backed into the bar to allow him through.

'Peggy, sorry, I didn't know you were, eh, standing there.' He removed his cap and stood beside her with it in his hands.

'Michael,' Jerome said. 'How are you? A bit early to be having a sneaky one, no?' He made covert drinking signs with his hands and winked at the young guard. 'Or are you in to see the telly? We don't actually have a licence for it yet, but, eh, I'll be straight on to it in the morning. Might as well make sure the thing works first, eh?'

149

Peggy shook her head.

'Right. Eh, no.' Garda O'Dowd coughed. 'Although you will need a licence for it of course. Oh, how are ya, Hugo? Didn't know you were back.'

'Just in, Michael,' Hugo said from behind the bar.

'Right, right. Very good.'

Peggy looked questioningly at him, and for a moment Garda O'Dowd simply smiled back, twisting his cap in his hands all the while, not moving from the door of the bar.

'So?' she said at last. 'Did you need something, Michael?'

'Oh right. Yes. Yes.' He coughed again. 'I am here on official business.'

'Yes?'

'Yes. Eh, I'm looking to bring someone in. For questioning.'

It seemed obvious to Peggy that, other than perhaps at home in front of his shaving mirror, Garda O'Dowd had never uttered these words before.

'Who?' Peggy asked. 'One of us?'

'Eh, no. Coleman Quirke.'

'Coleman Quirke?' Peggy almost laughed. 'Sure what could you want with Coleman Quirke?'

Garda O'Dowd's hands dropped a little, as if he might be wondering the same thing himself. He cleared his throat again. 'Detective Sergeant Ryan wants to ask him some questions. Up at the station.'

'Frank wants to question Coleman? So it's about the body? You think Coleman might have something to do with the body?' Peggy heard Maura gasp.

'Eh, I'm not at liberty to declare what Detective Ryan wants to speak with Mr. Quirke about. And', he stood a little straighter, 'might I say that it's of no concern to you. Or anyone else.'

Peggy noted his tone. She was almost impressed with it. But she wasn't about to let Michael go at that. It was her bar he was standing in, after all.

'Sure didn't he talk to him on Friday? Here at the bar?' Peggy pointed over to where Jerome was standing, the forgotten television instructions open on the counter beside him. 'Couldn't he have asked him his questions then? What's the point in dragging an old, sick man off to the station, making a holy show of him in front of the likes of Bernie O'Shea and the rest of the auld biddies who will be only too delighted to jump to conclusions?'

She stopped. She wasn't sure why she was defending Coleman as she was. They all knew he was in the toilet. He'd have to come out eventually. But something made her hope he stayed in there long enough that Michael O'Dowd was gone when he did reappear. Bloody Michael O'Dowd. And bloody Frank Ryan. Who did he think he was, swanning into Crumm, causing mayhem, making totally unfounded accusations against crotchety old men? What could Coleman have to do with the body of a young girl? Sure didn't she have some other man's army tags on?

Peggy started to feel desperately uneasy. She just wanted Michael to be gone. Let Hugo and Jerome talk to Coleman, if he ever came out of the toilet. Let them sort it out. He was taking an awfully long time in there. Peggy tipped her head from Jerome to the door and back again. She glared at him, willing him to go out and look for Coleman. But then she thought about the man standing next to her, holding his cap in his hands. She guessed pretending not to know that Coleman was in there might be an offence, and Jerome had had enough trouble with the Garda already.

Then her deliberations were moot, as the door to the toilet opened, and Coleman appeared, looking like he had eaten something very bad, or had not slept for days, or both.

'Arrgh,' he said, holding his stomach.

'Coleman Quirke,' Garda O'Dowd threw a stern look at Peggy, and put his cap back on his head. 'I'd like you to accompany me down to the station. Detective Sergeant Ryan would like to ask you a few questions.'

Coleman looked up from where he stood, supported by the doorjamb. Peggy thought it was genuine surprise that she saw on his face. Then he held his stomach again and groaned. He lunged for the bar, grabbing an upright to stop himself collapsing to the ground. Jerome rushed to him, and helped him up onto a stool. The old man leaned forward on the counter and groaned again.

'Are you all right, Coleman?' he asked.

'Arrgh, sure I haven't slept. I've been wandering around the lake all night.' He took off his cap and held his head in his hands. 'Sure how could I sleep?'

Garda O'Dowd tentatively approached the bar, as if he was unsure as to how to proceed. Peggy pushed herself past him and went to Coleman. She looked over his bent white head at her brother. Jerome just shrugged.

'Coleman,' Peggy said gently.

The man shook his head.

'Coleman.' She spoke with what Jerome called her 'time, lads' voice. This more forceful pitch seemed to resonate with Coleman, and he shied away a little from her.

'Coleman. Look at me.'

Coleman groaned again, and tilted his head a little towards her. Then his eyes met hers, and he froze for a moment, before groaning again and turning his face to the counter once more.

'Coleman,' Peggy pleaded. But before she could say anymore, the front door opened again, and Detective Sergeant Frank Ryan let himself into The Angler's Rest.

TWENTY

It was a strange group of individuals that congregated in Casey's Bar on that Sunday morning, late in September 1975. Frank hadn't expected the bar to be open at all, and yet here he was, standing inside, with six pairs of eyes on him. Within seconds, he realized that he didn't know two of them, those belonging to a small, grey-haired woman sitting at a table to his right, and those of a dark-haired man, similar in age to himself he guessed, standing behind the bar. The man looked a lot like Jerome, but heavier, older. More serious. He lacked the sheen his brother seemed to exude. Frank noticed Peggy's cheeks were almost the same colour as Garda O'Dowd's, who looked at Frank as though he had caught him with his hand in the station biscuit tin.

'Sir,' Garda O'Dowd began.

Frank put up his hand to stop him. He walked over to the bar. 'You must be Hugo,' he said, extending his hand over the counter. 'I'm Detective Sergeant Frank Ryan.'

'Hugo Casey, Detective.' Hugo shook his hand. 'I've heard a lot about you.'

Frank noticed both Jerome and Peggy glare at their brother. Then they all looked up as the door into the house opened suddenly behind him, and Carla came into the bar. A wide grin spread across her face as she scanned the room.

'Aw, how sweet,' she said. 'Everyone's here!'

Frank decided to ignore her. He turned very deliberately towards Peggy. 'Ms. Casey,' he said. 'I realize this is your place of business. But I was hoping to have a word with Mr. Quirke here.'

Peggy looked from Frank to Coleman and back again.

'Mr. Quirke,' Frank addressed the back of the man's head. 'Mr. Quirke, I'd like to ask you some questions. About the discovery of the body down at the lake on Thursday last. It won't take long if you cooperate. I can ask you them here of course.' He took an exaggerated look around the barroom. 'But you might prefer if we did it up at the station.'

Coleman raised his head just an inch, and addressed Frank from between his fingers. 'What is it you want with me?' he cried. 'First that fool,' he jerked his elbow in the general direction of Garda O'Dowd, 'now you. What is it you think I've done? I've done nothing!' He sounded as though he might actually weep. 'Nothing! Oh,' he groaned again. 'If you only knew. I've done nothing!'

Frank was a little taken aback by the man's outburst. He looked around him. He would prefer not to have to drag the old man out into the street. He knew his theories were only that … theories. The man might be telling the truth, and have nothing whatsoever to do with the girl found at the lake. But he was acting very strangely. More so, Frank suspected, than usual. He looked over at Maura.

'Maura has worked with us for fifteen years,' Peggy said, apparently reading his mind. 'She's like one of the family. You can say whatever you like in front of her. It will go no further. Jerome,' she turned to her brother. 'Lock the door. Let no one come in until Detective Ryan has got what he came for. If he wants to ask Coleman some questions, let him ask him them here. And Coleman,' she addressed the pitiful heap bent over the counter, 'you will answer him. Truthfully. Or you will not be welcome here at Casey's from this day on.'

The room stood still. Even Carla was silent. The old clock on the wall ticked four times before Jerome went over and pushed the bolt across the door.

'Now, Detective,' Peggy said, 'what is it you have to ask of Coleman?'

Of all the places Frank had questioned suspects in a murder investigation he had to admit that The Angler's Rest was the most unorthodox. He pulled a high stool over and sat down at the bar next to Coleman.

'Mr. Quirke,' he said, gesturing at Garda O'Dowd to take notes. 'Mr. Quirke. Before the dam was built, you and your brother, Desmond, you were both farmers. Is that correct?'

Coleman tilted his head a little towards Frank, but said nothing.

'You farmed the land in the valley? Before the dam was built?'

'What has that got to do with anything?' Coleman said gruffly. 'Yes. Yes, we were farmers. Cattle farmers. Is that it? Oh, Lord, but I'm tormented.'

'But after that, after the dam was built, and the valley was flooded, you found other work. Isn't that correct, Coleman? Mr. Quirke? You worked as a postman for the Post and Telegraphs from 1951, until you retired in the late sixties. Yes?'

'So what if I did? Didn't I tell you as much the other evening, here, sitting at this very bar?'

'Well, Mr. Quirke. You may be aware that the body found on the shore of the lake last Thursday evening was stuffed into a postbag: a jute Post and Telegraphs post bag from the early Fifties.'

Frank heard Maura gasp behind him. He wished this conversation were taking place in the privacy of the Garda Station. There might be no connection at all between Coleman and the sack used to hide the body. But he might know of how such a bag could have got misplaced, or mislaid. Who else might have had access to them? Who else worked for the P&T in the area in the early Fifties? Frank was far from being convinced that this old man had committed any crime. Having said that, his English colleagues had yet to track down his old girlfriend in Stowe, which is where she had allegedly moved to. And the body had yet to be properly dated. Frank needed to keep his mind open to all possibilities and all potential leads. The postbag was only one.

'Oh Mother of God,' Coleman moaned into the counter-top. 'Ye have no idea. I'm tormented.'

'Mr. Quirke. Do you know something about the body at the lake? Is there anything you can tell me that might help me find out who she was? How she got there? Coleman? What do you know?'

'What's tormenting you so, Coleman?' Peggy asked him. 'If you know something, tell Frank. Tell us. Coleman. Tell us.'

'Oh Mother of God,' Coleman cried. 'He squeezed the bridge of his nose between two fingers. 'Mother of God.'

Garda O'Dowd took a step towards Frank. 'Eh, perhaps, sir, it might be more appropriate to bring him in.'

Frank knew Garda O'Dowd was right. Coleman was acting increasingly suspicious. He clearly knew something about the body, and they weren't going to get it out of him in Casey's. Frank knew what had to come next. But he also knew that he didn't want to upset Peggy; Peggy, who he had been thinking about half the night as he had lain awake beneath the haunting gaze of the Sacred Heart picture on his bedroom wall. He hadn't really noticed it the first night at O'Shea's, he had been so exhausted, but last night it had stared down at him with a look of such disappointment he found he couldn't sleep. Lying there, he had tried to think about the woman whose bones were probably decomposing on some sterile gurney up in Dublin; a woman he had never met, and yet who now depended on him to find her truth, to tell her story. But his thoughts had kept returning to Peggy; Peggy, whose life was also being snuffed out by the lake in Crumm, albeit in a less obvious way. For some reason, he felt he owed her. He didn't want to upset her any more than he had to.

'Coleman,' he said quietly. 'I don't want to have to arrest you.'

'Ah Jaysus,' Jerome started, looking to Hugo for support.

Frank spoke urgently. 'I don't want to go down that road, Coleman,' he said into the old man's ear. He smelt earthy, an odour of stout and turf and old age. 'I don't want to do that. But if you won't answer my questions, I'll have no choice.'

Coleman looked up at Frank as if he might be mad. 'Arrest me?' he said. 'Why would you want to arrest me? Sure I had nothing to do with it. I didn't put her there.'

'Who did, Coleman?' Frank knew he was taking a chance, but something told him to persist. 'Who put her there?'

'Oh Mother of God.' Coleman held his head in his hands again. 'Sure I don't know. But sure it must have been himself. Oh Lord. I can see it now. He must have done it. Oh sweet Mother of God.'

Frank put his arm out to stop Garda O'Dowd from coming any closer. 'Who was she Coleman? What was her name?'

None of the others spoke. Hugo and Carla stood still behind the bar. Peggy had her hand over her mouth, her eyes wide.

'Murphy,' Coleman said in a whisper. 'Bernadette Murphy. Her father owned the mill in the village. The one … the one you saw, out in the middle of the lake. Holy Mother of God. It's so long ago now. So long ago.'

Frank realized he had been holding his breath, and he released it in a long sigh. Bernadette Murphy. He thought of the sunken face, frozen in death on the table in the sacristy. Bernadette Murphy.

'Holy God,' Peggy whispered. 'But Coleman. Who was she? And … and how do you know? How can you be sure that it's she?'

Peggy's eyes told Frank what he himself suspected. There was only one way Coleman could know. And that was if he had put her there himself.

'Coleman,' she said. 'You … you didn't?'

'I did nothing!' the man cried. 'I've already told you. I did nothing!'

'Eh, sir, Mr. Quirke should perhaps be put under arrest?' Michael O'Dowd leaned in closer to Frank. 'He should, perhaps, have a solicitor present?'

Before Frank had a chance to agree, Coleman lifted his hands in the air either side of his crusty ears.

'No, no. Listen to me. It was last night. When you said about them army tags.' He half looked at Peggy, who flushed and glanced at Frank. 'You said she was wearing metal army tags. Maxwell, you said. And do you know, I'd forgotten.' He shook his head. 'I'd actually forgotten, all this time. Well, we had been told to forget, so we did, I suppose. You did what you were told back then,' he murmured.

Jerome looked as though he was about to speak, but Frank raised his hand to quiet him. He knew from experience that, once someone started telling their story, once they started remembering, it was best not to interrupt them. It was best to let them speak.

'What had you been told to forget, Coleman?' he said.

'Her father owned the mill. Back before it was flooded.' Coleman spoke quietly, his eyes tightly shut, almost as if he was telling himself a story. 'Her mother was long dead. 'Twas just herself and the brother and the father. They ran the mill on the river.' He looked up at Hugo who was standing over him on the far side of the bar. 'You could bring a fleece to them back then, and they'd make it into a blanket. Or the makings of a shirt.' He seemed a little calmer now as he spoke, his hands out before him on the bar, remembering back generations to a time when the landscape of the area was very different. 'He was a good man, Murphy. He worked hard, himself and the son. She, the Lord have mercy on her, she was wild. What with having no mother, and the father worked every hour God sent. Oh Mother of God,' he broke down again, covering his face with his hands.

'What happened to her, Coleman?' Frank spoke with authority. He didn't want to spook the old man, but he needed him to keep talking. 'Do you want a drink, Coleman?' He nodded at Hugo. 'Maybe a cup of tea?'

'No, no,' Coleman cried, shaking his head hysterically. 'It was the year before the dam was finished. There were army boys here, checking the buildings, the bridges. I told you,' he turned suddenly

158

on Frank. Then his eyes met Peggy's and he groaned again and looked away.

'They were setting out the explosives,' Frank prompted. Hugo left a glass of water down next to Coleman. 'They were getting the place ready for the flooding.'

'Aye, aye.' Coleman ignored the water. 'And they had other army boys here. Americans. Explosive experts.' He spat the word out. 'They were … they were stationed up north after the war.'

Frank raised his brow at Garda O'Dowd, and the young guard started scribbling frantically in his notebook.

'That fellah,' Coleman said. 'Maxwell. He was one of them.'

'One of who?' Frank asked.

'One of the American lads. He was here in 1951, he was involved in blowing up the farm, the mill, all of that. He was one of them.' His face contorted as if the memory was causing him actual physical pain. He looked up at Frank. 'We wouldn't have known who he was, only that young lassie kept going on and on about him. He that left her his tags.' He jabbed his elbow in Peggy's direction, but he wouldn't look at her. 'Those tags young Peggy was talking about. Oh she wore them like they was diamonds. She'd be in Grogan's, or off down the bleachers, and she'd have them on, and be going on about her American soldier, and how she would be going to live in New York with him. Oh, she never stopped. They used to say she was touched,' he tapped his finger to the side of his head. 'Oh, but I don't know. I don't know. I think she really believed she would.'

'So what happened to her?' Peggy blurted out, before biting her lip.

'Oh, what happened, sure what always happens, the oldest story in time, he went back off up north and back home to America no doubt, and left her here, and the next spring she had his child for him.'

The three women in the room gasped. Frank had forgotten that Maura was still sitting behind them at the table.

'And I don't remember,' Coleman went on, agitated. 'Sure weren't we all being turfed out that year, moved on. Her father and brother moved on up to Dublin. Everyone had to get out that year. But she stayed. She lived up the bog road past Ballyknock. I remember, because herself and the little babby were living out there, all on their own. I don't know how she survived. I used to see her the odd day with the post. She must have been less than a year there.' He rubbed his forehead gruffly.

'But I know they came back. Them army boys. They came back in the summer of 1952 to see the dam being closed and the start of the flooding. I remember that well, because old Mr. Grogan wouldn't serve them, and there was trouble about that. And then, she left.'

'Who left?' Carla said.

'The Murphy child. Bernadette. She disappeared off with her army fellah. Well, sure, wasn't that what we thought at the time? She had been so excited to see him back, and then when the army left, she was gone. The whole village just assumed she was gone with him.' He stopped again and looked up at Frank and Peggy. 'Oh sweet Mother of God,' he said, and started keening over the counter.

'Coleman,' Peggy put her hand on his back. 'Coleman?'

But Coleman kept rocking forward and back, muttering something Frank couldn't make out.

The he turned to look at him again, startling them both.

'But sure how were we to have known? Didn't it make total sense that she had gone? And when she didn't take the child with her, it was just assumed that they were starting a new life in America.'

'But all the while, she was lying dead in a postbag under the water of the lake.' Jerome turned to Frank. 'And if he killed her, and buried her in the fields around the mill, he would have known that the water wouldn't be long covering her up.'

'He probably had a wife and kids back in America,' Carla added. 'The fucker. He probably just wanted rid of her. No hard work for a big soldier.'

Hugo suddenly turned away from them, and stood, staring into the mirror behind the till.

'It was just assumed she was gone with him,' Coleman repeated. 'No one had any reason to think otherwise.'

'The poor girleen.' Maura's voice was broken with emotion.

'So what happened to the baby?' Peggy said.

Suddenly the room seemed very still. Coleman stopped rocking and sat with his eyes fixed to the counter before him. Jerome stood, eyebrows knitted, like someone trying to work out a very difficult puzzle. Frank could see Peggy's reflection. Her face was pale, her gaze on the back of Coleman's head. He caught Hugo's eye in the mirror, and they stared at each other for a moment.

'Yeah,' said Carla. 'What happened to the baby? If they didn't go to America?'

'You said she didn't take the baby, Coleman.' Peggy's voice was steady. 'You said that everyone had assumed that they'd left to start a new life without the baby.'

Coleman started muttering under his breath again.

'Coleman?'

'Your mother, Mrs. Casey. She took the baby in.'

Coleman looked up at them all. 'Carla was only a year, and she said that she would take the child in. She didn't want to see her being taken up to any orphanage in Dublin or wherever. She said she and your father would take her in as their own. A Casey. The curate here at the time, he had worked in those orphanages. He knew what they were like. He said it was the right thing to do. He made us all agree not to speak of it again.'

Jerome turned away from the bar, but then swung around again. 'You're a fecking liar, Coleman Quirke,' he said, his eyes blazing. 'You're making all of this up. You,' he pointed at Michael. 'Arrest him, for fuck's sake. He obviously had something to do with that girl's death.'

Frank saw that silent tears were coursing down Carla's cheeks. Maura got up and stood behind Peggy, her hands on her shoulders, glaring at Coleman.

'You don't know what you're talking about,' she started, her voice raised. 'What are you saying, Coleman Quirke? Sure, you're only an auld drunk. How could you remember all of that? Sure, you wouldn't remember to get up in the morning, only Desmond is there to wake you.'

'It's all true!' Coleman swung around in his stool. 'Every word of it! You must remember that half the place left that summer. It wasn't so difficult to hide a secret like that. Most of the village would have thought that she left with the child, gone up to Dublin. Her father had disowned her when she got in the family way, and he was long gone by then. I myself only knew the whole truth because of my work delivering the post. I was around every other day. I could see for myself what was going on. And when Father Welsh told us that it was not to be spoke of, well, back then we used to heed the priests. Not like nowadays.'

'You're a liar,' Jerome shouted.

Frank noticed that he didn't look at Peggy, or attempt to touch her, but stayed on the other side of Coleman all the while.

'Hugo,' Jerome said. 'Throw him out. If the guards won't do it, well you and I surely can.'

'He's right.'

For the second time that morning, time seemed to stand still in The Angler's Rest. Hugo turned and Peggy locked eyes with her older brother.

'He's right,' Hugo said again. 'I remember.'

'What?' Jerome dropped his clenched fists.

'I remember, Peggy,' Hugo said to his sister. 'I was four years old. I remember Mammy taking you in. I remember the priest. They thought I was too young to remember, and they were right. I … I didn't.' He looked earnestly at Peggy. 'But now … now I do. Mammy had you on her lap in my old blue blanket. I remember, I remember not wanting you to have it. But Mammy said you were a gift from God. A special new Casey, given to us to love. She said you were my sister and … and you were. From that day on. My sister. Our sister.'

162

Frank watched Peggy's expressionless face stare at Hugo across the bar. He wasn't sure, but it looked like Maura might be bearing her weight. He extended his arms towards them just before her knees seemed to buckle under her.

'Peggy? Peggy? Are you okay? Peggy?'

Carla reached across the bar to her sister, but Peggy suddenly stood up straight, elbowing Frank and Maura's supporting arms away. Coleman stayed bent over the bar, as if his own demons were already too much for him to bear, as if he couldn't bear to look at her, but the rest of them just stared, gaping at Peggy, Hugo's revelations like a solid thing in each of their mouths, preventing any words being formed. Peggy's gaze fell to the floor for a moment.

And then she bolted. The sudden movement surprised Frank, and before any of them could react, Peggy had reached the front door of the bar, flung across the lock and disappeared outside, sending the door crashing against the wall of the porch in her wake.

Frank locked eyes with Jerome for a second, and then he looked at Garda O'Dowd. 'Stay here,' he ordered, pointing at Coleman's rocking frame, and without another word himself and Jerome ran out of the pub.

Outside, the sun blinded him. He stopped and scanned the area, but there was no sign of her.

'The lake,' he heard Jerome say, and Frank turned and raced after him down the track he had walked with Peggy only the previous afternoon. The two men ran without speaking. There was no sign of her ahead, and Frank was beginning to worry that they were running in the wrong direction, when they suddenly reached the shoreline, and he could see the form of a woman running on ahead of him over the muddy silt, long black hair trailing after her.

'The burial site. She's going to where the body was found,' he panted, and he slowed his pace.

'Jesus,' was all Jerome could manage.

The two men were now walking, Jerome just a little ahead of Frank, their sights firmly set on Peggy who had now also stopped running, and seemed to be half walking, half stumbling to the place where she and Frank had stood less than twenty-four hours before. They watched as she got closer to the site where the silt was still disturbed, a long narrow indentation in the sand that had held the broken body of a young woman she had never known, a woman long forgotten. They watched as Peggy fell to her knees only a few feet away from the place where her mother had been concealed from her for so many years, the place where Peggy's truth had been squashed into a jute postbag, and left to be forever entombed by the water of the lake.

The sight of her splayed on her knees in the sand made the two men start to run again, but there was a sudden rush of colour and flying hair, and Carla sprinted past them both towards Peggy. She fell to her knees on the sand beside her, dragging her sister's languid body to hers, cradling her like a baby. The sight made Frank's stomach contract. He longed to go to Peggy and hold her too, but he paused a little away from where the women were, leaving Jerome to walk slowly towards them. The place hadn't changed since he had been here with Peggy a day earlier: the same eerie stillness hung around him like a threat, the water in the lake dark and menacing even under the sun, which still beat down from the unremittingly cloudless sky.

The scene was made all the more distressing by Peggy's silence. No wailing, no crying, no screaming was to be heard. She was simply thrown in Carla's arms at the edge of the shallow grave; their bodies rocking slowly to and fro. Frank realized that she would be in shock. He was in shock himself. He felt the uneasiness of someone who just simply didn't know what to do, and Frank was unaccustomed to not knowing what to do. He watched from a few feet away as Jerome stood over the two women, his hands in his hair, shaking his head as he stared down into the disturbed sand at their feet. Then a noise from behind Frank made him turn, and he saw Hugo striding towards them. He never took his eyes from his siblings as he walked past Frank and straight to where

Peggy was. Without a second's hesitation, Hugo crouched down, put his arms around Peggy, and gently lifted her from the sand. Frank stepped back a little, and watched as Carla and Hugo, with Peggy supported between them, made their way back towards the shore, where Frank could see Maura standing with her hand to her mouth. Jerome lingered a moment longer, before casting a vitriolic stare at the lake and all around it. The he turned and followed his siblings back across the sand.

TWENTY-ONE

Thursday, 5th June 1952

Hush, hush little one! Mammy's here. And Daddy's coming! It'll be all right now, my darling. We're not long for this godforsaken hovel. You and me, my love, we'll soon be on our way across the ocean, yes, on a big boat, my love, across the ocean to America. You'll be an American girl, my little Peggy. Just like Peggy Lee. Isn't that right, baby girl? Oh little Peggy, it is a good day, just like Peggy Lee said. Look at the sunshine? And Daddy is coming, and we'll soon be away from this wretched place. You are destined for greater things, my love. Wait until Daddy sees how beautiful you are. We're going to America, my sweet, away from Crumm, and Ballyknock, away from all the people that don't love us, Peggy. Far away from the mill, and the blown up houses, and the empty fields. Let them drown the lot, little Peggy, it's all the place deserves. We won't be here to see it.

Here we are. Hush now, alanna, Mammy won't be gone long. Nice Mrs. Brady will mind you and I'll go and bring Daddy, my love. Oh just wait until he sees you. He will love you so, just like I do, my precious girl. Now, how does Mammy look? Am I nice? Daddy once said that red suits me – do you think Mammy looks nice, my love? His two beautiful girls, that's what he will call us, Peggy. His two beautiful girls. Oh, I love you, alanna. Be good until I come back with Daddy. And then we will be on our way to America, the three of us together, my darling. Be good now, Peggy. Mammy won't be long. I love you, my sweet.

TWENTY-TWO

'So I will be back up tonight, but it'll be very late.' Frank looked at his watch. 'After midnight at this rate. I just wanted to let you know. I'm sorry Rose, but there was nothing I could do about it.'

'No, no Frank. I'm sorry. I shouldn't have been nagging you. It's your job. Of course you had to stay down. I understand.'

Frank's heightened senses picked up on the note of desperation in Rose's voice. No doubt her mother had been advising her to back off. Not to run the risk of scaring her Detective Sergeant away before she had her claws inextricably into him. But then he felt bad. It wasn't Rose's fault. He could hear the line forming in his head already … it's not you, it's me, but he knew better than to have that particular conversation standing behind the bar of The Angler's Rest.

'So I'll see you tomorrow?' The line crackled loudly. 'Or whenever,' she added with extra emphasis. 'You'll give me a call?'

'Yeah.' Frank moved closer to the wall to allow Jerome to pass behind him. 'Sure. Okay. Bye Rose.'

He replaced the handset and stood for a moment, watching Jerome flick metal caps off two mineral bottles with one hand before plonking them on the bar.

'Woman trouble?' Jerome said without turning his head.

'Eh, no. Not really, no.' Frank could hear how unconvincing he sounded.

Jerome grinned at him over his shoulder. 'See?' he said. 'You're better off without them.' And he walked around the other side of the bar and lifted the drinks he had prepared, winking at Frank before turning and bringing them over to a table where two middle-aged couples sat, laughing amicably. Frank saw the couples smile at Jerome, the men patting him on his back, the women making jokes about how one of their daughters was still single and wouldn't herself and Jerome make a lovely couple. Jerome laughed it off, oh, sure who would want to marry a publican, wasn't it a terrible life. Frank watched him standing there, running his fingers through his silky hair, chatting with his customers. He was a natural, Frank thought. He'd do well with a bigger place up in Dublin.

Jerome picked up some empty glasses and came back around the bar. Some sort of truce had evolved between them over the course of the afternoon, and Frank felt at least that Jerome had taken him out of his sights for the moment. Even if his finger was still on the trigger.

'Will you have something?' Jerome tipped his head towards the bar taps.

'No. No, thanks. I'll drive back this evening. I'd better keep a clear head.'

'You'll be against the traffic at least.' Jerome opened a bottle of Coke and poured it into a glass. 'Kerry are some outfit.'

'They are.'

'They'll be celebrating that for a few weeks.'

'They will. They will.'

The two men stood next to each other, looking out over the bar, both talking about football, when Frank knew that they were both thinking about Peggy.

It had been some afternoon. Frank had put his own expertise to good use by staying in the bar while the family had taken a very shaken Peggy inside to the house. Frank wasn't sure exactly what had gone on there, but when a red-eyed Carla, face bloated from crying, had come back into the bar to fill a glass with brandy, he had heard guttural sobs coming from the kitchen beyond. By then he had dispatched Garda O'Dowd to the station with a list of calls to make to Dublin Castle and Washington. He had almost felt excited for the boy as he went off, full of his own importance, to carry out the first proper police work he had ever probably had the opportunity to do. Hugo had already driven Coleman home to get some rest.

'They're banging on the door to get in,' Frank had said to Carla.

'Well, let them in so,' she had said indifferently, and had gone back inside the house to comfort her sister.

Her sister.

Frank could hardly get his head around it himself. Standing behind the bar alone, he thought he knew the right thing to do. Not as Detective Sergeant Frank Ryan, but as Frank Ryan, friend of Peggy Casey and the extended Casey family.

So he stood on a table and pressed the button. And on it came. The grass was as green as any field he had driven past on his way to Crumm on Friday afternoon, just two days before. And there they were. Dotted around the pitch, each man facing the tricolour, the Artane Boys Band playing 'Amhrán na bhFiann', and the sound of sixty- thousand voices with them.

Frank had hopped down from the table and surveyed the scene before him. A country pub, a family pub, warm, comforting, welcoming; an establishment any publican could be proud of. And up high in the corner, on a dark wooden shelf, the All-Ireland football final, Dublin versus Kerry, about to begin.

Frank had heard a tap- tapping on a glass pane, and had turned to see someone peering in the window next to the porch. The face was smiling, and pointing up at the television. Then there was another bang on the door, and Frank had turned and opened The Angler's Rest for business. Halfway into the first half of the match, Frank had found that he simply couldn't cope. Such was the interest in the game, that it seemed most of Crumm and half of Ballyknock had arrived and were drinking bottles of orange and Cidona, and pints of shandy and plenty stronger. Every stool had a posterior on it. When Frank had spotted the red curls of the O'Malley kid whom he had met down at the lake gravesite, he had beckoned him behind the bar.

'Keep your eye on things for a minute,' he had said to him, and had gone through the door to the house, leaving the boy gawping, terrified behind the counter. Frank had tapped on the door at the other end of a short, dark corridor lined with boxes of Tayto crisps and paper serviettes. Hugo had answered it.

'I need you and Jerome in here,' Frank had said, and Hugo had nodded. Behind him, Frank could see the backs of Maura and Carla, their arms around Peggy, leaving the kitchen through a far door.

'She's going for a lie down,' Hugo had said and Frank had just nodded.

After that, the three men had worked all afternoon, feeding the punters pints and crisps until the crisps ran out and the final whistle blew, and Frank decided that they could cope, leaving the pub to go and check on Garda O'Dowd back at the station.

Now he was back, and things had calmed.

'Thanks for today,' Jerome turned to Frank. 'I mean, this afternoon. And well, just, thanks.'

Frank nodded at him. 'You know, Jerome,' he said. 'If your friend has any trouble in the future. With any of the boys up in Dublin.' He glanced at Jerome to see if he understood. 'Let me know. You can mention my name. Anytime. If I can help you, well, I will.'

Jerome looked as if he didn't really believe Frank, but hadn't the bad manners to say so. 'Thanks,' he said, and turned away.

The place had emptied out now. Most of those in for the match had left for home and their dinners after watching Pat Spillane raise the Sam Maguire for Kerry. The usual Sunday fare of baked ham and vegetables had not been served in The Angler's Rest that day, and if anyone had noticed, they hadn't said anything. The television had been distraction enough. Frank walked back around into the bar towards where Carla and Maura sat with Peggy harboured between them. They had stopped drinking tea now, and had moved on to glasses of cider after Carla had announced that she couldn't stomach another cup and that they all needed something stronger.

As Frank approached Peggy's table, he was a little thrown by the warm smile Carla gave him.

'Here he is. Sit down Detective Sergeant.' She pulled a stool over between herself and Peggy, and moved to allow him space to sit. 'Here's a man who's done a full day's work.'

Frank searched for a hint of sarcasm and was genuinely shocked to find none.

'Are you back up to Dublin tonight? Sergeant?' Maura smiled across the table at him.

'I am,' Frank said. Peggy kept her eyes on her glass and said nothing.

'Well, you'll be against the traffic at least,' Maura said knowingly.

Frank smiled. 'I will,' he said. 'I will.'

The four of them sat in silence. Frank could see *The Waltons* had started on the muted television.

'Well,' Carla said at last, 'Maura and I were just going inside to make a few sandwiches.'

'Oh no, I couldn't eat,' Maura started. 'My stomach is still sick.' Carla glared at her.

'Oh yes!' Maura said, laughing nervously. 'You know, I'd ham baked this morning. I'll slice it up and sure couldn't we all have some of that on brown bread?'

'You'll eat something before you leave, Frank,' Carla said and put her hand gently on his.

'Thank you, Carla,' Frank said. 'That would be great.'

172

'Right so.' Carla stood and waited until Maura did the same, then she ushered her away from Peggy and Frank, towards the bar and the door into the house.

They sat at the little round table in silence, Peggy never moving her hand or her stare from her almost untouched glass of cider; Frank leaned over, elbows resting on his thighs, hands clasped between his knees, his eyes never moving from her face. No one approached them, and Frank could sense Jerome's protective guard up, watching them, ensuring they weren't disturbed. They sat for what felt to Frank like a long time.

'I'm sorry,' he said at last.

The shadow of a smile pinched Peggy's lips.

'Maxwell,' she said.

Frank said nothing.

'That's my name.' She looked up at him for the first time that evening. 'Peggy Maxwell. Not Peggy Casey. Peggy Maxwell.'

Frank knew that none of it was his fault. But he also knew that it was very likely Peggy would blame him anyway. For now. Everything had been fine until he had arrived. And now … now this young woman's life had been totally turned upside down. Until the passing of time gave her a clearer perception, she would blame him. And Frank knew that the best thing he could do for Peggy right now, was to let her.

She looked back at her glass. 'My name is Peggy Maxwell. My family were the Murphys who ran the old mill that's under the lake. And my father murdered my mother when I was only a few months old.'

Her voice was calm and steady. It unnerved Frank a little. It didn't sit well with the red eyes or the pale, blotchy skin that told him a story of trauma and upset. But then she looked up at him and his heart broke to see no mania in her lovely eyes, only utter sadness. She reached out and took Frank's hand and held it on the table between them.

'I'm not angry', she said, 'with you. You probably think I am. That I blame you. I don't. At all.'

She stared at their hands on the table. Once again Frank knew he was crossing a line between Frank Ryan, Detective Sergeant, and Frank Ryan, the man, but the pull was too strong, and he squeezed her fingers gently in his.

'I just need to say it out loud,' she said. 'I can't with the others.' She glanced quickly at the bar, and then back to their clasped hands. 'I can with you.'

They said no more for a moment. Frank summoned every bit of willpower not to look towards Jerome who he knew must be staring at them, sitting there, holding hands. He suspected Jerome would think Frank was taking advantage of Peggy. He concentrated on not looking up.

After a minute he spoke. 'Peggy, we don't know for certain yet what happened to … to Bernadette,' he said in a low voice. 'I realize Coleman's story sounds plausible. But we don't know for sure. Not yet.'

Peggy smiled through watery eyes. 'But you know she was killed, Frank,' she said. 'She was murdered. She was buried in a sack.' She kept her eyes on their entwined hands. 'Is he still alive?'

Frank knew what she was asking. 'Yes,' he said. 'He's living in New Jersey. His wife,' he stopped suddenly. He knew he had to be gentle. 'His wife is dead. But he has children. In the States. And grandchildren.'

'Wow,' Peggy said. Her eyes were wide, as if she was trying to understand it all, to take it all in. 'You can find out a lot in a few hours, huh?' She gave a weak laugh.

Frank noticed that she didn't ask him about John Maxwell's other family. Her half-brothers and sisters. That would come later, he supposed.

'Washington were able to trace him fairly quickly based on the dog tags. And Hugo's connections helped too.'

'Hugo's connections?'

'Well, working in the Irish embassy. It has its benefits. They can apply a little pressure. Get things done faster. He made a call and, well, it helps.'

'Hugo works for the Irish embassy?'

Frank could see that this was news to Peggy.

'Eh, yeah. He seems he's quite senior there. In London.'

Peggy just laughed a little laugh, and went back to looking at Frank's hand in hers. 'It seems all the Caseys have secret lives so,' she said. 'Who would have thought it?'

Frank's hand was starting to feel hot and sweaty, but he didn't want to move it from Peggy's. He sat, fighting the urge to put his arms around her and hold her there at the table. He could pretend all he liked that he was just there in his capacity as a member of the Garda Síochána, but he knew it was a lie. He thought hard about what he would be saying to another person in her position. Someone he didn't think he was falling in love with. He coughed, and used the opportunity to take his hand from hers, leaning in a little closer to her as he did.

'Peggy,' he said softly. 'They will arrest John Maxwell today. He will be questioned about Bernadette Murphy and his time here in Ireland. In Crumm. You realize … you realize that he must have known about you all this time?'

Peggy just stared at her glass and nodded.

'They will want to question you. In Dublin, most likely,' he went on. 'And Coleman, of course. And Hugo.'

Peggy just nodded again.

'I want to bring her home,' she said suddenly. She looked into Frank's eyes. 'My … my mother. I want to bring her home to Crumm. She should be buried here. Properly buried here.'

'Of course.' Frank made a silent promise to himself and to Peggy it would happen. And he also promised himself he would be here with her for it. If she wanted him to be.

'The family that left,' he said. 'The Murphys?'

Peggy shook her head emphatically, startling Frank by her sudden movement.

'No. No,' she said. 'I can't think about them right now. They left her here. They never came to look for her. No.'

Then she turned in her seat a little and looked up at the row of rusted relics hanging above the bar.

'The loom. I told you? It came from the mill.' She stared up at the innocuous piece of metal nailed high above her head for years without her being aware of how significant it was. It looked to Frank like something you might find in the bottom of an untidy toolbox, and yet that piece of the mill was the closest link Peggy had to her real past.

Her real family.

Her truth.

She kept her eyes trained on it. 'Do you think she's at peace now?' she said in a whisper.

Frank swallowed, and reached over to take her hand in his own once more. 'I do,' he said. 'I do.'

Then they heard footsteps on gravel, and the sound of laughing voices got louder outside until the door of the bar swung open. Then four, six, eight smiling men stood inside. Frank recognized Fergal Maher.

''Tis like a morgue in here!' One of the men exclaimed, a wide sunny smile on his face, which he directed at Peggy. 'Did ye watch the match, lads? They made some job of poor Mickey Ned, wha? Them Dublin boys? What a day, huh? What a day for Kerry. The cousin played a blinder!'

Within moments, it was as if someone has flipped a switch on The Angler's Rest, and life pulsed through the bar again. Two of the men went to sit in the corner and started to unpack musical instruments they had brought with them, while the rest of the men stood talking, finding stools, calling to Jerome for pints.

Frank was wondering if he should bring Peggy back into the kitchen and away from all the noise, when she surprised him again by pulling her hand gently from his, and standing up. She smoothed her hair back and tied it with a rubber band she took from her wrist.

'Lads. Ye must be starved after the journey. Will ye have

sandwiches with those pints? We can't have our customers complaining that they weren't fed. Not at Casey's Bar.'

'Good girl, Peggy.'

'Oh that would be grand, Peggy.'

'Go on the Caseys.' The few men standing at the bar who had got their drinks first raised their glasses in appreciation of her.

'Peggy,' Frank stood behind her, speaking quietly into her ear. 'You don't have to do this. You should go inside to Carla, no? Maura can sort these lads out?'

Peggy turned to him. He looked and could see many things in her eyes. Defiance. Hurt. Anger. But he could also see love. Trust. And hope. He prayed silently that the hope had something to do with him.

'I am a Casey,' she said, her eyes shining, her voice breaking. 'This is my bar, my family's bar. My father's bar.' She took Frank's hand and squeezed it quickly. 'This is my home. And I have customers that need looking after.'

And then the music slowly started and grew until it filled the ears of everyone in The Angler's Rest, and Peggy Casey walked past smiling faces and friendly nods back towards the place she knew she truly belonged.

Acknowledgements

Sincere thanks to Catherine Ryan Howard, Hazel Gaynor, Helen Bovaird Ryan, Vanessa O' Loughlin, Eoin Purcell and Clodagh Burghold. Thanks also to Ger Nichol, Sarah Hodgson and everyone at Killer Reads. With particular love to my fabulous family and friends.

KILLER READS

DISCOVER THE BEST
IN CRIME AND THRILLER.

SIGN UP TO OUR NEWSLETTER FOR YOUR CHANCE TO WIN A FREE BOOK EVERY MONTH.

FIND OUT MORE AT
WWW.KILLERREADS.COM/NEWSLETTER

Want more? Get to know the team behind the books, hear from our authors, find out about new crime and thriller books and lots more by following us on social media:

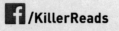 /KillerReads    /KillerReads